OLIVER CRUM AND THE BLOOD SEEKERS

OLIVER CRUM BOOK THREE

CHRIS COOPER

DREADFUL
MEDIA

Oliver Crum and the Blood Seekers

Published by Dreadful Media

Enjoy the book? Please consider leaving a review at goodreads.com or amazon.com. Every review helps. To receive news of new publications, events, and exclusive offers, please sign up for the Dreadful Media Newsletter on our website.
WWW.DREADFULMEDIA.COM

CHAPTER ONE

Fluffy white flakes drifted from the overcast sky in large clumps. Izzy and Oliver stood on the front porch while Pan ran through the yard, trying to catch the icy treats in his tiny corgi maw. Whenever he caught one, he would chomp victoriously, only to realize moments later it had mysteriously vanished.

"First snow of the season," Izzy said, taking a deep breath. "You can smell it in the air."

"I think that's the sauerkraut you're smelling." Oliver crinkled his nose. "Who makes sauerkraut for Thanksgiving, anyway?"

Izzy put her hands on her hips. "First of all, we agreed to refer to the holiday as A Day of Remembrance for our Exploited Native American Brothers and Sisters. And I grew up eating sauerkraut every year. It's a German thing."

"Can we at least come up with an abbreviated name? ADRENABS, maybe? Sounds nice and pagan."

Izzy sniffed the air again. "No time. The pie's burning." She turned and rushed inside.

Oliver took one last deep breath of the chilly winter air. A cold front had come roaring in early on this Thanksgiving Day, cutting fall several weeks short and covering Christchurch with a thin layer of bright snow.

A blast of warm air hit Oliver as he stepped through their front door. The oven had raised the temperature on the first floor by several degrees as dishes went in and out for the better part of the day. As he let Pan in behind him, the snow clinging to the pup's fur quickly melted, leaving droplets on the floor as he scurried to the kitchen.

Asher was sitting on the sofa, head buried in a paperback.

"Didn't you smell the pie burning?" Oliver asked.

"Oh, sorry," Asher replied, eyes darting up from his book. "Just got to the part where he battles the windmills, and I have a feeling it will not end well." He set the book on the coffee table and stood.

"I thought you were peeling potatoes," Oliver said.

"Already peeled the whole bag. Aren't other people bringing potatoes too?" He smirked. "We'll have enough to feed Christchurch ten times over."

"Has no one ever explained the power of leftovers to you? They're what *Thanksgiving* is all about." Oliver smiled while whispering "Thanksgiving" so that Izzy wouldn't hear. He unzipped his coat and hung it on a hook next to the door.

"Saved it," Izzy said, returning triumphantly from the kitchen with Pan on her heels.

Nekko, Oliver's butterscotch tabby, waddled in behind them, carrying a jumbo marshmallow in her mouth.

Oliver pointed. "Someone doesn't want to wait for dinner. Might want to take that from her."

Izzy turned and sighed. "At least she's not sticking her nose in the casserole dishes like last year. Let her have the marshmallow."

"She is a marshmallow," Asher added, "with tiny little legs."

"You're going to give her a complex," Izzy replied as she bent down and struggled to pick the tabby up.

After a few heaves, she gave up on lifting the cat, and Nekko took the opportunity to sneak under the sofa to consume her stolen treat in private. Pan stuck his nose under there but knew better than to follow.

They headed to the kitchen to cover the last of the casserole dishes and pie tins for transport to the town hall.

"You do this every year?" Asher asked, looking at the plethora of food scattered around the room.

"Well, this is the first year we're all getting together at the town hall, but eating until you can't see straight is something Americans like to celebrate all year round. Today's the only holiday dedicated to it, though," Oliver replied as he pulled a length of aluminum foil free from the roll.

"Let's not forget the important tradition of spending time with all your least favorite family members and arguing about politics," Izzy said. "Speaking of, how's your mom?" She grinned.

"Be nice. I talked to her yesterday, and she's decided to spend the holiday on a Caribbean cruise. She told me she was taking my advice and trying to see more of the world. I'm sure she'll spend most of her time reading on the deck, but at least she's trying."

"That's spontaneous of her," she replied.

More than a month had passed since his mom, Bev, had stood in the living room, brandishing a kitchen knife. Oliver could still hear the guilt in her voice when they spoke of the incident over the phone although he held nothing against her. The Siren's song had been too strong for anyone to resist, including Anna. Still, he was happy the events had brought them closer together.

Although his relationship with Bev came packed with years of baggage, it had vastly improved of late. Ruby, on the other hand, had become a ghost since he last saw her in The Parlor's courtyard, standing next to the makeshift grave of her lost love. She'd promised to check in, but they'd heard nothing from her for the last month. He could tell the radio silence bothered Asher although the man refused to talk about it.

"Need some help with those?" Asher asked Izzy as she struggled to lift a bowl containing an entire bag's worth of mashed spuds.

"You think I'm weak, don't you?" she asked. "I'll have you know I may be old and have arthritis, tennis elbow, and carpal tunnel, but I can lift a bowl—"

She gripped the sides of the dish and tugged, trying to lift it off the counter. After several failed attempts, she nodded for Asher to take it.

"Not a word," she said.

Pan lay underfoot, diligently waiting for dropped scraps.

"Anybody home?" Anna shouted from the front door.

"In here," Izzy replied.

Anna stood at the kitchen doorway, a pie dish cradled in one hand and a bottle of wine in the other. "I see you three have been busy. It's roasting in here."

She set the pie plate and wine on the table and took off her coat. "Thought I'd stop by and see if you needed any help. Dad dropped me off on his way to the hall. He sends his regards and wishes you all a happy Thanks—" She looked at Izzy.

"Day of Remembrance for our Exploited Native American Brothers and Sisters. It's really not that difficult," Izzy replied.

"Right... that. Anyway, Dad says hello."

"How is he?" Izzy asked. "Still fighting with the council over next year's budget?"

"He doesn't like to talk about his mayoral duties when I'm around, but the Elders are giving him a hell of a time. Every time I see him, he's grown more gray hair. Think he's even considering retiring from the political life. He told me to let him know if you have any openings at the bakery." She smirked.

"Ha! Could you imagine?" Izzy asked.

After wrapping the rest of the dishes, they loaded the station wagon and piled in for the short drive to the town hall.

Cars lined the edges of the square where Izzy pulled the car onto the main road next to the market. She found a vacant spot near the town hall, and several Christchurch townsfolk emerged from the building to help unload.

"Martin, good to see you," Oliver said, opening the trunk.

"You too. And Happy Thanksgiving!" Martin replied. He pulled a few pies from the baking racks stacked in the back.

One Elder held the door open as they rushed inside to escape the cold, the sidewalk salt crunching under their feet.

The town hall had been completely decked out for the holiday. Round tables draped with fabric table-cloths replaced the normal rows of wooden folding chairs, and cornucopia centerpieces sat on each table, overflowing with decorative gourds. Autumn wreaths hung along the walls, interspersed between filigreed orange-and-yellow banners.

Oliver spotted Madeline, the Elder leader, across the room as she waved them over to a vacant serving table.

"Happy Thanksgiving," she said as they approached.

"You too," Izzy said, refusing to say the name of the holiday aloud.

"You can set all the desserts on this table, and I'll get started opening the wine. Oliver, could you give Martin a hand with the coolers next to the front door?" Madeline asked.

"Will do," Oliver replied although Madeline had already turned her attention to another table.

Martin patted Oliver on the back. "So how's it been?" he asked, pointing him toward the front of the hall.

"Oh, pretty good," Oliver replied. "Find any exciting antiques for the shop lately?"

Martin ignored the question, but once they were out of Madeline's earshot, he leaned close. "Haven't seen anything strange—you know—at the edge of the woods, have you? Haven't seen any of *them*?"

"Not a lot of action down that way," he replied. "Seems like Briarwood's keeping to itself. I still see a bit of smoke now and then but no people. It's hard to see through the trees, though. I can just see tops of buildings."

Oliver bent down to grab a handle on a cooler, but Martin stopped him short.

"I know this may sound odd, and Madeline would kill me for even asking, but if you ever think of going back there, I'd be happy to join. You could be my guide."

"Martin, if I go back, you'll be the first to know, but I can't see that happening soon."

"I know, I know," Martin replied. "But just imagine the living history! If they really haven't been outside the woods for centuries, think of what we could learn.

If word ever got out, we'd have people coming in from all over the world to study the place."

"That's if the people in Briarwood don't try to kill us first. The less attention Briarwood gets, the better."

"Forgive me. It's just not often—ever—that a history fanatic has the opportunity to see history firsthand."

Martin lifted the other end of the cooler, and they carried it to one of the serving tables.

Since the Briarwood dome had broken, little more than a month prior, Martin had been overly eager to see the once-hidden town up close. Fortunately, the rest of Christchurch treated Briarwood as they had treated most other unsavory realities—with metaphorical earplugs.

Oliver hadn't been honest with Martin, though. Although the Briarwood residents were mostly keeping to themselves, on one occasion, he had seen a figure at the edge of the woods. He'd tried to convince himself the sighting was a figment of his imagination, but Gideon's lumbering form was hard to mistake for an old tree stump. While tending to the bees one day, Oliver had seen the man standing just on the other side of the crumbled briars.

Once they had finished with the coolers, Martin leaned close once more. "Good to see you, Oliver, and think about my suggestion," he said with a wink before stepping over to Madeline. "Need help with anything else, love?"

"A glass of red wine," she replied. "And save me a seat. I'll be over in just a minute."

Martin watched her with adoring eyes as she crossed the room to the mayor, who was in the middle of an epic story and at the center of attention of a group of men. He gestured wildly as the others in the circle let out deep belly laughs.

After waiting a moment or two for a story break that never came, Madeline tapped the mayor on his shoulder and pointed at her watch.

He excused himself from the group and took the podium at the front of the stage then tapped the microphone until the talk died down to a low hum.

"If everyone would please take their seats, I'll make it quick, so we all can enjoy the delicious spread." He gestured toward the serving tables, loaded down with dishes of all shapes and sizes.

Oliver sat with Izzy, Anna, and Asher at a table near the center of the room.

"I'd like to start by thanking everyone for joining us today and for bringing their best dishes to share. Also, a special thanks to the Elders for organizing such a fantastic event."

The crowd applauded, and Madeline blushed, giving a dismissive wave to the audience.

"When the suggestion of a town Thanksgiving crossed my desk, I have to admit that I was skeptical at first. But considering the *eventful* year we've had, what better way to celebrate today than by giving thanks together? So please... eat, drink, and if you end up a little too merry, make sure someone else is driving you home."

The crowd chuckled as the mayor raised his glass. "To Christchurch," he said.

"Here, here!" a few men in the crowd shouted as everyone lifted their glasses high.

Although the townspeople were usually prim and proper, all bets were off when the crowd descended upon the food. Oliver was standing in front of Asher in line, watching his expression as he shuffled toward the row of impressive turkeys sitting glazed and glistening on a serving table. Another table had been entirely dedicated to various forms of spuds.

Oliver returned to his seat after scooping a piece of Izzy's apple pie onto his plate. Fortunately for the town, Izzy had spared them from the tofurkey she'd made the previous year.

Asher sat down with a heaping plate of food so heavy that the table wobbled a bit when he set it down.

"First time at a buffet?" Oliver asked him.

"I couldn't stop myself."

The feast began, and after fifteen minutes of voracious eating and drinking, most of the townsfolk filled themselves to capacity and leaned back in their chairs.

"I'm going to die," Asher said.

"Mission accomplished," Izzy replied, winking and tipping her toothpick in his direction.

"Mission accomplished only once you've had dessert," Anna added.

Asher's eyes widened. "I couldn't."

"Dessert *is* an obligatory part of the holiday," Oliver said.

After another hour of socializing, the townsfolk trickled from the hall into the chilly winter air and back to their houses. Luckily, all were insulated by bellies full of Thanksgiving food.

Izzy's tires whirred on the icy road as she drove back to the house. After everyone shuffled inside, Oliver made the mistake of heading to the kitchen for a glass of water. As he stood there, overwhelmed by the amount of dishes that still needed washing, Izzy approached from behind.

"They'll still be here tomorrow," she said.

"Looks like the snow is really coming down now." Anna stood next to the living-room window. "Didn't know it was supposed to be this heavy."

Oliver peered out the kitchen window. Although the snow had started with sporadic flakes, it was coming down much more quickly and had already accumulated to nearly an inch.

Izzy emerged from the hallway closet in a heavy winter coat. "Let's go out back. Nothing like a fresh snowfall."

Oliver bundled up and headed out to the back porch. Pan squeezed through the door as soon as it opened wide enough and took a running leap off the porch steps into the snow. He dragged his nose through the white fluff as he ran, trying to collect as much snow in his mouth as possible and forming an icy wizard's beard.

Izzy had wrapped the beehives in black plastic, leaving enough room for the bees to come and go but preventing cold drafts from seeping through the hives. The rigid forms looked like miniature monoliths poking through the snow.

Oliver looked out into the woods across the field. The Briarwood townsfolk had been trained to avoid the briars for so long that he doubted anyone would attempt to cross. In the few weeks since the Siren's attack on the town, he'd planned to venture to the woods, to see what had become of the secret community, but memories of his last visit overpowered his curiosity.

A snowball hit Oliver square in the cheek, sending

a cold chill down his chest as bits of ice trickled into his shirt.

"What was that for?" He spun around.

Izzy stood giggling. "First snowball of the season! Had just enough to scrape one together—although still a bit too powdery, in my opinion."

As Izzy did a victory dance with Pan prancing around her feet, Oliver tried to cobble together another snowball but had little luck, and the awkward clump broke up in the air before reaching its intended target.

"You'll never beat the master," she added.

"On that note—think I'll be going in," Anna said from behind Izzy. "Gotta get back home soon anyway."

Asher emerged from the back door, having missed the impromptu snowball fight.

"Want a ride? We can take the wagon," Izzy said.

"I'll just walk," Anna replied.

"You're nuts. Come on. Let me take you home," Izzy said.

"Aw, you're worried about me?"

"More worried about who'll replace you at the bakery if something were to happen to you." Izzy grinned.

"Funny." Anna walked toward the back door as Izzy followed. "See you all tomorrow."

Oliver spotted two lids from a set of old metal trash cans tucked against the house.

"Ever been sledding?" he asked Asher.

Asher gave him a puzzled look.

Oliver grabbed the lids and gestured for Asher to join him in the yard.

"Won't Izzy need these?"

"The cans are empty. Izzy used to store birdseed in them, but blackbirds overran all her feeders, and she stopped buying seed. These should make decent sleds," he added, handing Asher a lid.

"Sled?"

"Yeah." Oliver considered how to describe exactly what sledding was. He held the lid firmly out in front of himself. "Get a running start and slide down the hill on the lid. I used to sled all the time as a kid. We don't have this much snow in November very often, so we might as well make the most of it."

Asher looked down the snowy hill to the field below. "Are you sure this is a good idea?"

"You'll be fine. It's a lot of fun."

"What exactly am I supposed to do again?" Asher turned the metal lid over in his hands.

"Watch."

Oliver took a running start, pressed the lid tightly against his chest, and leapt onto the snow, landing on his belly as the lid hit the ground. His body bounced to the side, but he corrected himself as the sled picked up speed. The last time he'd gone sledding, on the big hill next to his childhood home, he wound up running into a tree. He kept *that* detail from Asher.

Oliver made it to the bottom, and the metal lid ground to a halt. He turned around to see Asher still standing at the top.

"Come on!" Oliver shouted.

"I think I'll just watch," he replied.

"Live a little."

Asher tried to mimic Oliver's approach, pressing the lid against his chest and leaping onto the hill. Instead of gliding elegantly, he overshot his mark, went face-first into the snow, then tumbled end over end to the bottom. He lifted his head out of a snow pile, face dusted with flakes, and laughed.

"The Russian judge gives you a five out of ten," Oliver said.

"What does that mean?" Asher asked.

"It's not important." He assumed Briarwood had never seen the Olympic games.

Oliver helped Asher up. "Not bad for your first try."

"I would hate to see what 'bad' looks like," he replied, brushing himself off.

"Want to go again?" Oliver asked.

"I guess I can't do much worse," he replied as they climbed.

As they turned toward Izzy's house, Oliver heard a

snap from the tree line behind him. Most of the leaves had fallen, leaving only barren branches lined with heavy, wet slush. Something moved at the edge of the woods, a flash of red in a sea of gray forest.

The first time Oliver saw Gideon had been a month before, a week after the Briarwood barrier broke, exposing the hidden city on the other side. Gideon's lumbering figure walked the edges of the tree line.

Out of all the people, why would Gideon have ventured to the edge of the woods? This time, however, Oliver was certain the hulking figure was the same person who had saved him from the Witch in the town square—a debt he had never repaid. Oliver felt tremendous guilt at having left the man behind, his dead sister lying on a cold dungeon floor. He could have ventured back to the town, but the chaos he'd glimpsed from the edge of the woods the month prior was enough to deter him. Still, if Gideon was a survivor, perhaps he had helped the town establish some order.

"What are you staring at?" Asher asked from halfway up the hill.

Oliver turned around. "Nothing." When he turned back to look at the tree line, Gideon had disappeared.

The snow came down harder as they made a few more rounds on their makeshift sleds. Eventually, Oliver's gloves soaked through, and he had a hard time gripping the edge of the metal lid with his numb fingers.

"Let's go back inside," he said after Asher had taken another haphazard trip to the bottom of the hill.

As they climbed, boots sinking into the snow, Asher turned to Oliver. "I've seen them, too, you know."

Oliver tried to play dumb. "What? Seen who?"

"The men at the edge of the woods. One's a gigantic fellow with a large sword, and the other carries a bow."

"Why haven't you told me?" he asked.

"That's what you were staring at, wasn't it? I could ask you the same question." Asher paused. "What if they cross over?"

"I've never seen the guy with the bow. You probably don't remember, but Gideon was there the night we found you in the cell."

Asher thought for a moment. "I remember. He was with you and the woman who..." Asher looked down at his shoes.

"His sister, Mercy," Oliver added. "But if it's really him, it means he's alive and well and maybe even has control of the town. After the coup, anyone could have taken over Briarwood, so we'd be lucky if that were the case—I think."

"I just hope they stay put for now."

Oliver did, too, and although he tried to rid his mind of the idea, he was certain Briarwood would come knocking one day. In some ways, he was surprised it hadn't already and just hoped the town had a long memory of the invisible barrier separating them from the outside world. Gideon could surely see Izzy's house from the edge of the woods and must have at least considered exploring the mysterious structure at the top of the hill.

As Oliver reached the back door, Anna smirked at him through the window.

"I thought you were going home. What's so funny?" Oliver asked as he stomped off his boots on the deck.

"Got caught up watching you two sled, but I was just about the head out. Nice tumble, Asher."

Asher blushed. "It was my first time." He sat down at the kitchen table to take his boots off.

"Well, Izzy and I enjoyed the show. And don't worry about it—the last time I went sledding, I broke my arm, so you've done much better by comparison."

"Why didn't you tell me it was so dangerous?" he asked Oliver.

"It's not *dangerous*. Some people are just uncoordinated." He stuck his tongue out at Anna.

"Ready to go?" Izzy asked, car keys in hand.

"I'll take her," Oliver said, reaching for the keys.

"It'll be fun to see how well the wagon handles the icy corners."

Izzy pulled the keys away from him.

"Just kidding. I'll get her home in one piece." Oliver took the keys and headed out to the car with Anna.

"How about a nightcap?" Izzy asked Asher before Oliver shut the front door.

"Not a bad Thanksgiving," Anna said as they climbed into the car.

Oliver started the engine and flipped the heater to full blast. "I can't say I was particularly excited to spend it with the entire town, but I enjoyed it. Watching Asher sled was the icing on the cake."

Anna laughed. "I guess today was technically his first Thanksgiving."

"You're right. I doubt they had a grand Briarwood Thanksgiving celebration, and if they did, he was probably locked in the cell. Still feels surreal, no matter how many times I say it." Oliver paused. "I haven't told Izzy, but I've seen Gideon twice now at the edge of the woods. We saw him tonight when we were sledding."

Anna perked up in her seat. "Why didn't you tell me? Did you talk to him?"

"I'm sorry. I didn't want to worry you for no reason and wasn't sure it was him until today. We didn't speak, but he was walking the tree line like he was looking for something."

"But that's good, right? If he's survived, then the town must be doing well."

"That's what I've been thinking. At some point, we will have to go back, or Briarwood will come marching up the hill. They have to figure it out eventually, right? That the briars are dead? We might as well be the first to act."

"I don't know," Anna replied. "Maybe when Asher is up on his feet and finds his own place. But I can't imagine it going over well with Gideon or the townspeople if they figure out Asher is living right across the way."

"But Gideon isn't like that. He saw Asher—saw what his father had done to him. If Gideon and his friends truly are in power, Asher should be safe."

He steered the station wagon down the path to Anna's cottage and parked in front of her door.

"Why poke the bear is all I'm asking," Anna replied. "Maybe they want to be left alone."

Oliver shrugged.

Anna laughed to herself.

"What's so funny?"

She hesitated. "Promise not to laugh."

"Promise," he replied.

"I've been taking self-defense classes in Amberley.

I just figured, after what happened with the Siren, we should prepare ourselves. Between Briarwood and whoever was pulling Simon's strings, it's only a matter of time, and we don't want to be caught off guard."

Oliver looked down at his lap. "You're right. Maybe I've been too lax. Just trying to keep a sense of normalcy is all."

"Normalcy? Since when have things ever been normal around here? Especially since you arrived." She jabbed him in the ribs with her elbow.

"Stay warm," he said as she climbed out of the car.

"Be careful on your way back. Seems like the storm is getting worse."

Oliver waited until Anna made it safely inside then turned the car around and drove back toward the square. The townsfolk must have been hibernating, wrapped up safe and sound in warm blankets, tucked away in their quaint houses in a town that had once promised unparalleled safety, security, and comfort.

Without streetlamps lighting the winding road to Izzy's, Oliver struggled to see through the flurry of snowflakes bombarding his windshield and cutting short the path of the headlights.

He parked under the porte cochere and braced himself for the cold as he made the short dash to the door. Once inside, he found Asher snoozing in the reading chair and Nekko taking up most of his lap.

"I'd say he's down for the count," Izzy said, still sitting at the kitchen table.

"Don't think I'm far behind him," Oliver added. "How do you drink coffee so late in the evening?" He eyed an empty bottle of Irish cream on the counter. "Oh, never mind."

"Hey, today is a judgment-free day."

Oliver laughed. "Well, I'm turning in. See you in the morning."

Izzy held up her coffee cup in a silent cheers.

Oliver climbed the stairs to his bedroom on the third floor. Nekko followed closely behind, her butterscotch flub swaying back and forth. Since Bev was off sailing the Caribbean, Asher had taken the other bedroom.

Although having his room back was nice—especially given the several occasions he'd hopped out of bed and directly onto Asher's stomach—he missed having the human company.

Oliver changed into his pajamas and moved his sketch pad aside as he climbed under the covers. He'd made a habit of drawing a bit before bed but gave himself a pass for the evening. He'd started sketching the events of the last year and had filled the pad's pages with drawings of the Witch, Simon, the Siren, and the no-longer-hidden town on the other side of the briar patch. Given the Siren's grim warning, he needed to release the stress of the situation. He was unsure of what evil forces would come knocking on Christchurch's door, but sketching seemed to release the pressure that would often build up behind his eyes and prevent him from resting peacefully.

CHAPTER TWO

O liver awoke to the sound of tires whirring in the driveway and pushed Nekko off his chest as he climbed out of bed. He peered out the window and saw the rear of the station wagon fishtailing under the porte cochere as Izzy tried to back out into the driveway. After the car nearly ran into the support column, Izzy gave up and pulled it back underneath. The snow must have been at least a foot deep and had completely covered the road into town.

Oliver threw on a sweater and jeans, ran his fingers through his hair, then walked into the hallway.

Asher poked his head out from his bedroom door. "What's that noise?" he asked.

"Spinning tires. Izzy's just trying to pull the car out of the port. You coming to the bakery today if we can get the car out?"

Asher no longer needed to hide from the people of Christchurch since the entire town knew of his existence. While he mostly cleaned dishes and helped with odds and ends around the bakery, he seemed to enjoy his new freedom and took any opportunity to escape the confines of the house after exhausting its supply of books. Christchurch didn't have a library of its own, but Oliver could barter baked goods for novels with some of the better-read townsfolk.

"I'll be ready in five minutes," he said.

Izzy stood next to the kitchen sink, face flushed and unzipping her puffy coat. She looked like a skinny hot dog wrapped in a fluffy bun. Her hair exploded into a frizzy mess when she pulled off her wool cap.

"Having fun out there?" Oliver asked.

"A blast." She crossed to the coffeepot and poured a fresh cup, holding it tightly to warm her hands.

"Is it supposed to snow all day?" he asked.

"Don't know," she replied. "The cable's out, so I couldn't check the weather."

"The internet too?"

"Everything."

Oliver looked out the back window. A snowdrift had formed on the edge of the porch. "Well, guess there's really no need for a forecast. By the looks of it, the snow won't be letting up soon. It's awfully early in the year for this much snow, isn't it?"

Izzy sipped from her mug. "We had a storm like this around Thanksgiving once, but that was a decade ago. The shops in the square were closed for a week."

"I saw you try to pull the car out of the port. You will let me drive, right?"

"Everybody ready to go?" Asher asked as he entered the kitchen. He laughed when he saw Izzy's hair.

She scowled as she tossed Oliver the keys.

The three piled into the car as Pan watched sadly from the front window. He'd made a habit of perching on the bench under the bay window in the mornings although Nekko would occasionally usurp his spot, using her girth to knock him onto the floor.

Oliver gunned it over the mound of snow at the edge of the port, sliding backward down the drive and onto the main road, nearly overshooting into the field on the other side. "See, just had to give her a little gas," he said as he shifted into drive.

"I'd rather make it to the bakery alive," Asher chimed in from the back seat.

Oliver went light on the pedal as the tires struggled to grip the snow at first, and he squinted to find the outline of the road. With the windshield wipers on high and the heater on full blast, he drove toward town, but navigating the flat layer of undisturbed snow in front of him was difficult.

"Think we'll get any customers today?" Oliver asked.

"No idea, but we've gotta try it. Remember the last time I closed the shop after Anna had already prepped for the day? She was furious." Izzy pressed a finger against the passenger window and drew patterns on the fogged glass.

Oliver exhaled as he pulled the car off the slippery snow-covered road and onto the paved street bordering the square.

"Tom must have plowed this morning," Izzy said.

Without enough roads to warrant an actual salt truck, the entire town depended on a man named Tom to hook a plow to the front of his pickup and clear the main roadways.

"Looks like they're going to open the market today," Oliver said.

The market owners were shuffling around inside although the bay doors were closed.

On the other side of the square, Martin was standing outside the antique shop, trying to set up his standing display in the snow.

"A bit surprised to see Martin out this morning," Oliver said.

"Don't you remember what day it is? The busiest shopping day of the year? The day the fat cats who own all the big shopping chains sit back and count their wads of cash." Izzy had worked herself up into a huff.

"Surely you're not talking about Martin. He's hardly the face of corporate greed," Oliver replied.

"Would you watch the road?" she said as the station wagon's tire rubbed against the square curb. "We won't do Anna much good dead."

Oliver corrected course. "I don't do Anna much good alive, at least when it comes to baking."

He pulled the car around the back of The Rolling Pin, and they braced themselves against the harsh wind as they struggled to reach the back door.

"Took you long enough." Anna grinned as she carried a set of dirty mixing bowls over to the kitchen sink.

"You should have seen Oliver round the bends into town. Have you ever seen Pan fly around the corners of the house and slide on the hardwood? Kinda reminded me of that." Izzy squeezed Oliver on the shoulder.

"I didn't see anyone else offering to drive," he shot back. "If it wasn't for me, we'd have had to walk here."

Oliver turned to Asher. "Want to help me open the front of the shop?"

"First, come here and try these." Anna leaned over a baking sheet on the large metal table. "Thought I would do something different and add candied orange rinds. Also mixed a bit of coffee into the icing."

Oliver looked over her shoulder at a tray of hot, gooey cinnamon rolls.

"Don't mind if I do," he said, grabbing a piece of a roll she'd cut into quarters.

"I think this is a winner," he said as the orange and coffee flavors hit his taste buds over the sweet icing. He'd never had the pleasure of trying homemade cinnamon rolls until he started working at the bakery—the ones from childhood always came from a can—and the perk was one he would never tire of.

The first few hours of the morning were slow as the storm raged outside. Oliver busied himself with refilling the napkin holders and cleaning the neglected nooks and crannies around the shop. By early afternoon, the snow had let up temporarily, and the sun even shone through the breaks in the clouds. Several customers trickled in as the day progressed.

Madeline and another Elder entered and sat at a booth in the corner of the shop.

Oliver rounded the counter with a fresh pot of coffee.

"Surprised you aren't out shopping today," Oliver said as he flipped over their coffee cups.

"We tried," Madeline replied. "Looks like the weather's causing issues with the train. We tried to make the drive to Amberley, but when we reached the edge of town, the roads were so icy we had to turn around, and the wind nearly blew us into a ditch. Lord knows when the county will clear it. Poor Tom's got his hands full as is. I'm sure those bums in Amberley won't be any help either."

"Be nice," said the woman across from her.

Madeline forced the corners of her lips into a smile. "You're right. We're just missing all the sales. I never miss Black Friday."

"I saw Martin opening up shop today," Oliver said, trying to change the subject. "Didn't know today was a busy shopping day for him."

"He's convinced he can pull in the Christchurch crowd since the trains are down. He says they need a place to shop. I told him to have at it. At least he's out of my hair for the day."

"Big plans, then?" Oliver asked.

"The rest of the girls and I are getting together later for cards and a few glasses of wine. What better way is there to keep warm on a snowy day?"

Oliver laughed. "Anything else I can get you two?"

"Two glazed donut holes, please," Madeline replied.

"Just two? You know they're tiny, right?"

"I want—" began the woman across from Madeline.

"The diet, remember?" Madeline shot a glance at

her. "The first bite of a donut is always the best. The rest are wasted calories."

"Whatever suits your fancy," Oliver replied.

The woman grumbled as he turned toward the kitchen.

Once Madeline and her friend had savored their minuscule treats, taking an unusually long time to consume them, they braved the tundra to Madeline's car, parked outside.

By late afternoon, the bakery was dead once again, and Oliver and Izzy had scrubbed every obscure surface, refilled every saltshaker, and even fixed the squeaky hinge on the front door, which had driven Oliver crazy since his first day in the bakery.

"I suppose we could close up shop early," Izzy said. She'd busied herself with dusting the bakery's artwork.

While the town had chosen traditional decorations for the month of Thanksgiving—autumn leaves, cornucopia, and miniature gourds—Izzy went for a different vibe. She had painted over Halloween's creepy mansion mural with a pop surrealist Thanksgiving dinner. The scene somewhat resembled the Last Supper although the people had been replaced with turkeys gathered around a serving platter holding a scared-looking human with an apple shoved in his mouth. His legs were trussed like a turkey, and his feet were capped with paper turkey booties.

Oliver tried to convince her to go with something less disturbing, and the painting did seem to garner critical reactions at first, but eventually, the clientele learned to ignore it, as they did many of Izzy's other eccentricities. Soon, Oliver would paint a new Christmas mural, and he'd settled on something more wholesome. Izzy had already come up with an alternative name for Christmas, but it was too lengthy to remember.

While they were cleaning up and closing the bakery down, a knock came at the front door.

"We don't have any pickups scheduled this afternoon," Anna said.

"I'll go see who it is," Oliver replied. He rounded the corner to the front of the bakery.

The stranger made another frantic *tap tap tap* on the glass, and Oliver had an unpleasant flashback of Simon tapping on the bakery door with the tip of his metal cane.

A thin silhouette was standing on the other side of the drawn blinds, and Oliver flipped the lock and pulled the door handle.

"Oh, thank God," the woman said as she huddled closer to the door, rubbing her exposed arms as the wind whipped against her dress.

"We've actually just closed." Oliver noticed her

gaunt face and deep bags under her eyes. "Is everything all right? Can I help you with something?"

"Just a moment to warm up before I head back out there, if you don't mind."

"Sure. The coffee should still be hot, if you'd like a cup." He opened the door wide to let the woman in.

"Awfully kind of you. I promise I won't be long."

Her flats slid awkwardly as she tracked snow across the floor.

Her dress was tattered and thin—an outfit that was no match for the storm—and although she was out of the cold, she continued to shiver as if the chill had settled deep inside her. She looked truly out of place against the hazy winter backdrop and appeared to have stepped in a deep snow pile since several clumps hung on the edges of her shoes, rubbing against her exposed ankles. She attempted to brush the snow off the sides of her flats but only wedged it deeper within.

"Take a seat," Oliver said as he turned toward the kitchen to grab the coffee pot. He returned a moment later and poured a cup. "Not prepared for the weather, eh? What brings you to town?"

She held her coffee cup tightly, trying to absorb its warmth. The woman pulled the glass sugar shaker closer and poured for an unusually long amount of time. "I have little time for small talk."

"Oh?" Oliver was taken aback by her bluntness.

She took a swig of coffee. "Do you know Asher? I have a message that I have to get to him."

The hairs on Oliver's neck stood on end. He tried not to let his expression show his discomfort.

"Um, no, never heard of anyone with that name," he lied. He eyed the back of the kitchen, but Asher was out of sight, probably leaning over the sink, doing dishes.

She rubbed a tear from the corner of one eye.

"Do you need for me to call—"

"No, no," she replied. "You can't. There isn't time, and it wouldn't work anyway."

"What's going—"

"Just listen!" she shouted, slamming the mug on the table and splattering coffee everywhere. "I have to find Asher. I know he is staying in this town."

"Oh," Oliver replied. "How did you get into town? Seems like no one's been able to get in or out today."

"I came in on the train," she replied.

"The train's up and running again?"

"I wouldn't say that. I was on the last train in. His train."

His train?

She slid out of the booth seat.

"Where are you going?" he asked.

She turned toward him and gripped his arm, bringing her face uncomfortably close.

"If you find him, tell him to find a safe place to hide until the storm passes."

Anna emerged from the kitchen. "Everything okay?" she asked, brandishing a wet dish towel.

"She's looking for someone named Ashton." Oliver had played this game before.

"Asher," the woman corrected.

"Oh, right. Know anyone named Asher?" he asked Anna.

Anna shook her head. "Nope. And in a town this small, pretty sure I'd recognize a name like that." She was the perfect accomplice. "You might look at the pub, though. They have a few rooms—maybe your friend is staying there." Anna pointed. "Just across the square, next to Fletcher Antiquities at The Horseman. You can't miss it."

The woman turned toward the door and stepped back out into the cold.

He walked toward the window and watched her stumble awkwardly across the square.

"What the hell was that about?" Anna asked.

"I don't know. Looked like she'd been through hell. I will give the pub a call—let them know she's coming."

"What did she want?" Asher asked from the kitchen doorway. "I heard my name and figured I should make myself scarce."

"She said she had a message for you: hide," Oliver replied.

Asher bristled. "That's creepy. Should I be worried?"

"I don't know," Oliver said as he walked to the phone behind the register and picked up the receiver. "Static. Forgot the phones are down."

"Seems like we've lost everything but the power. Surely the folks at the bar won't be dense enough to tell her where Asher is, you think?" Anna asked.

The woman had already crossed the square and was well on her way to the pub, wind whipping her tattered dress.

"I hope not. She said she came in on the train. *His* train. Who do you think she meant?"

Anna shrugged.

"I'll look at the train station," he said. "Would you go to the police station and tell Eric what happened?"

Eric, the Christchurch chief of police, had had his own firsthand experience with the unusual occurrences around town. His run-in with the Siren a few weeks prior left him temporarily her brainwashed thug.

"Will do," Anna replied.

"We'll wait for you!" Izzy shouted from the kitchen.

Oliver slipped on his pea coat and hat and stepped out into the cold.

He walked the path toward the station but, from a distance, saw little activity. Snow had covered the benches, and the place was a ghost town. As he walked through the archway, though, he saw a mammoth engine resting on the tracks next to the platform. Oliver had seen many types of trains pass through, but this black riveted beast looked more like a steam engine than a modern passenger or cargo train.

The locomotive's smooth metal sides gave the train the appearance of an austere bullet, perched on the tracks like a mobile fortress.

Oliver took the bridge to the other side of the station and stopped midway, looking down onto the top of the train. He stood silent for a few moments, hoping to hear someone else shuffling through the station but heard nothing more than the wind echoing through the stalls.

He looked for doors on the sides of the train cars, but all were shut tight. The two cars attached to the engine appeared to be passenger cars, but the windows had all been blacked out.

On his way back to the entrance, he noticed a light in the station office and stopped in to speak with the attendant.

"Any idea of where that train is from? It's odd looking, isn't it?" Oliver asked.

"I haven't seen a train like that in years," the attendant replied without looking up from his clipboard. "It's a private train."

"What's inside?"

"It's a *private* train, which means the contents are none of your nor my business."

"Thanks," Oliver said sarcastically.

The attendant seemed to sense Oliver's frustration and looked up from the counter. "Odd trains sometimes come through here. Could be on its way to a museum or to a tourist route. Won't be going anywhere for a while, though, not with this weather. Nothing's been in or out for hours and likely won't be until the storm passes. Can't get through on the radio to Amberley station to check their status either. I'll try again tomorrow."

As Oliver approached the bakery, he saw Anna entering the police station in the distance and looked across the square toward Martin's. *Maybe he'd know something about the train.*

The tent sign in front of Fletcher Antiquities had fallen over in the snow, so Oliver picked it up, dusted it off, and repositioned it closer to the building to protect it from the wind.

Every time he entered Martin's antique shop, the place seemed more claustrophobic than before. He often wondered if Martin made any money on the shop or if it was more of a personal collection than anything else.

Martin was sitting at his desk in the back of the store, head in hands until the jingle from the door caught his attention. He bolted up from his chair and raced to the front door.

"Oliver!" he shouted. "Come to do a bit of early holiday shopping? Great deals today. Izzy's been eyeing that boa over there—would make a perfect Christmas gift."

"Just had a question for you, Martin. Sorry to disappoint," Oliver replied.

"No worries," Martin said with a noticeable sag in his smile.

"Know anything about trains?" Oliver asked.

Martin cocked his head to one side.

"A girl wandered into the bakery this morning and said she'd come in on a train. She looked like she'd just crawled out of a dungeon. I went to the station to have a look, and the only train that's been in or out is still there, but it's not like anything I've seen pass through the station before."

"Cargo train, perhaps?"

"Maybe, but aren't those typically long? This one's only a few cars. It looks old, too, not like the modern ones that come through."

"You know, Harry's built a massive model-train

display in his basement. I've been helping him locate a few hard-to-find models. Can't say I know a lot, but tell me what it looked like."

"It's shaped like a bullet and has sleek lines and skinny windows. This sounds odd, but it kinda reminds me of Izzy's station wagon—like it comes from the same era."

"You don't suppose it could be an old steam engine, do you?"

"I thought it could be, but do they still use those?"

"You don't see them often, especially not one that old. But—something interesting—when I was helping Harry find a particularly rare model, I ran into someone who collects full-size train cars. Runs a museum out west. Perhaps it's going to a collector."

"Sounds like Harry's serious about his trains," Oliver said.

"He's got to keep himself busy. Still has music, too, but I think the trains help him keep his mind off Francis."

Oliver still saw Francis in his dreams now and then. He couldn't bring himself to sketch her, though, like he'd sketched the Witch or the Siren. The bodies were just too personal, too painful. He'd resigned himself to seeing them forever in his nightmares.

"Maybe a collector, then," Oliver said, snapping

back to reality. "You didn't see the woman walking by, did you?"

"I wish," Martin replied. "Aside from Madeline this morning, the place has been dead. She was right about opening up today—what a stupid idea."

The bell jingled against the door glass, and Martin perked up once more.

"Are you coming or what?" Anna asked from the entryway. "We're done at the bakery, and Izzy's ready to go. She saw you cross the square."

Oliver looked back at Martin, who tried to hide his disappointment with another forced smile. "Tell you what." He pulled his wallet from his back pocket and rifled through a thin stack of bills. "I don't have enough cash to cover it now, but I'll take the boa. If you could set it aside for me, I'll come back with the rest when I can sneak it back to the house."

Martin beamed. "Will do. At least I've made one sale today. Black Friday didn't go as planned."

"Stay warm, Martin," he replied as he turned toward the door. Once he and Anna had left the shop, he asked her, "Did you talk to Eric?"

"He said he'd head over to the pub and talk to her."

Izzy had warmed up the car and pulled in front of the bakery. Oliver climbed in the back with Asher, while Anna hopped into the front passenger seat.

Izzy pressed the pedal hard, and the car skidded around, doing a donut in the other direction.

"Easy!" Anna shouted.

Their station wagon garnered an odd look from a man loading groceries in his car in front of the market.

Izzy giggled. "Always wanted to do that." She eased off the pedal until the tires gripped the slick snow accumulating on the road around the square.

"So, any luck at the train station?" Izzy asked.

"None. I talked to the station manager, but he wasn't much help. With the storm, I can't imagine it's going anywhere soon."

Izzy steered back toward the square and down the road by the market. A fresh layer of powder had already covered the tire tracks from earlier that morning.

"Good thing I just had new tires put on a few months ago," Izzy said as she pulled into the driveway.

"What are you all up to for the rest of the day?" Oliver asked.

"I've got a new vegan chili recipe I've been dying to try," Izzy said.

"Yum," Oliver replied sarcastically.

"Don't knock it until you try it," Izzy shot back.

CHAPTER THREE

While Izzy and Anna busied themselves in the kitchen, Oliver took Pan to the backyard. The pup hopped to the ground from the bottom step of the porch and disappeared underneath a foot of snow, so Oliver grabbed the snow shovel from the garage and cleared a path for him.

After fifteen minutes of shoveling, when Pan's little corgi body began to shiver, Oliver opened the back door to let him inside. He turned toward the woods and noticed a smoky haze over the forest below.

Another fire. Things in Briarwood must not be going well. But as Oliver looked at the smoke, he realized it wasn't coming from Briarwood but blowing in from town. He rounded the house to the front yard. A column of black swirls was billowing from the side of the square.

Oliver rushed inside. "Come look at this!" he shouted. "Something's on fire near the square."

Izzy came flying in from the kitchen, wooden spoon in hand. "Not the bakery!"

"I don't think so. It looks like it's coming from Martin's side."

"We've got to get up there," she replied.

Asher tossed his paperback onto the coffee table. "Let's go."

Oliver thought of the woman's message and the Siren's warning from a few weeks before, and a knot formed in the pit of his stomach. "No, I think you should stay here."

Asher's look shifted from confusion to terror. "You don't think it's got something to do—"

"Just stay here. I'm sure it's fine," Oliver said, despite not being sure at all.

"Let me drive," he said to Izzy. Somehow driving made him feel as if he was helping.

"I'm not a child." Asher raised his voice as he stood from the couch, catching the others by surprise. "I'm going with you."

Oliver started to speak, but Anna cut him off. "He's right. He shouldn't stay here by himself." She turned toward Asher. "But until we know what's happening in the square, stay here, and I'll stay with you." She gestured for Oliver and Izzy to go.

Izzy and Oliver climbed into the car, and he drove as fast as he could to the square although the roads were icier with each trip.

"It's not Martin's," he said as they approached the square. "Looks like it might be the pub."

As he pulled around the corner, tall flames lapped up toward the sky, shooting red-hot embers and black smoke into the cold winter air.

A crowd had gathered around the burning building, and Oliver parked off to one side.

Eric stood in a tan trench coat, watching as fire consumed the building and frantically trying to reach someone on the other end of his police radio.

"Where's the fire department?" Oliver shouted as he approached.

"They'd have to come from Amberley, but the damned phones are down."

"What about the radio?"

"Static. I'm not sure how, but the storm must be interfering."

"But that isn't poss—"

Eric left Oliver hanging as something on the second floor caught his attention. "Someone's still inside!"

The crowd stood, hands clasped and mouths gaping, as Eric called over the two other Christchurch police officers, Will and Gary. A face appeared in a window on the second floor, a ghostly floating head surrounded by rolling smoke. Mitch, The Horseman's bartender, gasped for air as he hung halfway out the window, trying to catch the wind blowing through town.

"A ladder!" Eric shouted. "I need a ladder."

"There's one by the garden shed out back." Will rushed to the back of the pub and returned with a rickety wooden ladder.

Eric leaned the ladder against the window frame as the flames crept closer.

Mitch frantically grabbed for it, but his eyes seemed sealed shut by soot and ash.

Eric climbed the ladder and pulled him over the windowsill by the back of his charred shirt, guiding his hands to the top rung. The two other officers waited below and eased the man down to the ground.

Mitch lay in the snow, struggling to breathe and badly burned. He clutched his chest as Eric pulled the radio from his pocket and tried once more to reach someone, anyone outside of Christchurch. In a moment of frustration, he threw the radio to the ground and knelt next to Mitch.

"We can't wait here. We have to take him to Amberley," Eric said.

"I'll grab a cruiser," Gary said.

"They're snowed in. We don't have time for that."

Eric looked at Oliver and pointed at Izzy's station wagon. "Help me get him into the back seat."

Oliver looked at Izzy.

"Take him," she said. "I'll stay here." Her eyes were red and glossy as they darted between Oliver and the burning building. "Be careful."

The officers lifted Mitch gingerly and carried him to the back seat of the car. He let out a raspy scream as they slid him inside.

"You okay to drive?" Eric asked Oliver.

"Yeah," Oliver replied, heading toward the driver's seat.

"Keep working the radio," Eric said to the other officers. "Tell the hospital in Amberley we're on our way."

Eric climbed into the passenger seat, and Oliver floored it, at least as much as he could without losing control on the icy road.

Mitch wheezed as Eric twisted around to help him.

Oliver's eyes darted to the rearview mirror. He hadn't seen the damage up close but got a glimpse as Eric shifted out of the way. Spots of bright red were mixed with ash on Mitch's face, and the fire had completely burned off patches of his clothing.

"Mitch, buddy, you have to calm down. We're taking you to the hospital." Eric tried to keep the quiver from his voice, but it cracked as he examined Mitch's wounds.

Mitch slapped the back of Oliver's seat, and Oliver looked again into the mirror. The man's hair had been burned, and the fabric of his shirt seemed to have melted into his shoulders.

Oliver swallowed hard and focused on the road ahead.

He swerved past the Christchurch sign, trying to keep the car on the road by memory.

As they drove farther away from town, the snow and wind picked up.

"I can't see anything," Oliver said, but Eric was preoccupied with Mitch and ignored him.

The back seat grew eerily quiet. Oliver checked the rearview mirror, against his better judgment, and saw Mitch's arms had fallen against his chest, his head slumped to the side.

"He's stopped breathing," Eric said as he climbed into the back seat, bumping the steering wheel and nearly knocking the car off the road.

"I can't see where I'm going!" Oliver shouted.

The wind blew hard against the side of the car, causing it to shudder.

"Keep going. Come on, Mitch!" Eric straddled the burned man and started CPR.

The windshield went white, but before he could

slam on his brakes, and as he was easing off the gas, an object at the side of the road came from nowhere. He swerved hard, trying to avoid it, but clipped it on the station wagon's front bumper. The car slid across the road and into an embankment, sending Eric flying against a door and Mitch against the back of the car seats.

"What the hell are you doing?" Eric shouted.

"I'm sorry! I hit something."

Oliver tried to start the car again, but the engine refused to turn over.

While Oliver tried to start the engine, Eric continued to work.

After a few tense minutes, Eric stopped. "Shit," he said, wiping the sweat from his forehead with a coat sleeve. "He's gone, goddammit! He's gone." Eric opened the door and climbed out into the snow.

Oliver was frozen, trying to keep his eyes from wandering up to the rearview mirror and unable to comprehend how the lazy winter day had ended in a violent death.

"Get out here, kid." Eric stood by the driver's-side window and tapped on the glass, fury on his face.

Oliver climbed out into the storm, sinking into the snow halfway to his knees.

"You want to tell me why the hell you were driving around in circles?" Eric asked.

"What? I wasn't driving in circles," Oliver replied.

Eric pointed at the top of the embankment several feet behind the car. Somehow, Oliver had driven directly into the corner of the Christchurch welcome sign. The sign had sunk sadly into the snow, held up only by a loose bolt and one remaining crooked signpost. The other lay in pieces in the snow.

"We passed that sign," Oliver said defensively. "I swear I was driving straight toward Amberley."

Eric bent over and put his hands on his knees, taking several deep breaths as he tried to regain composure. "It's okay. The roads are terrible. It's not your fault." His breathing slowed. "Get in. I'll drive. We still need to get him to Amberley. We can't take him back like this."

As he climbed back into the car, Oliver refused to look at Mitch's body. A feeling of guilt washed over him, rising from deep within his belly until a wave of nausea hit his esophagus. He put his hands to his lips and swallowed. "I'm sorry. I swear we were heading in the right direction."

Eric turned the key, and with a bit of finagling, the engine turned over. The car slid and fishtailed as he tried to pull it up the side of the embankment. He drove to where the ground leveled out and got back onto the road.

The only sounds audible in the car came from

slush underneath the tires and violent wind whipping against the station wagon's frame.

Oliver's heart was racing. *How could I have been so careless? I've taken away his only chance by driving like an idiot.* He held in his emotions the best he could but wanted to roll down the window and scream into the storm.

The wind picked up once more, and a blast of snow made it harder to see. Eric tried to keep the car steady on the road, but soon they could see nothing but a blanket of white.

"Christ, you weren't kidding," he said.

After several moments of cautious driving, the Christchurch sign appeared once again in the distance.

"What the hell?" Eric said. He stopped the car to look.

"I told you I was driving in the opposite direction," Oliver replied.

"But that's not possible."

Oliver thought for a moment. "Did you find the woman? Anna told you, right?"

Eric shook his head. "She did. I went to check it out, but by the time I got there, the fire had already consumed half the damned building."

"So you didn't see her? She might be inside."

"Oliver, if she was inside, she's dead. There's no

way anyone would have survived the fire. You see what it did to Mitch."

Oliver looked at the burned man in the back seat. "This is it. The Siren said *he'd* be coming. Whoever *he* is, I don't know, but that woman was trying to warn us." He looked out into the storm. "We're trapped in Christchurch."

"But *who*? If we can't get out, how would anyone get in?"

"They're already here, I think," Oliver replied. "The woman said she came in on the train, but Madeline said the train station's closed. Went up there myself, and it's empty. But there's a train parked there —not an ordinary passenger train but an old one."

"Strange trains come through all the time. We had one painted like a clown pass through a few years ago."

"They've locked us in." Oliver started to panic. "How else can you explain it? The phone lines are down, no one can leave, and the radio doesn't even work. Radios don't just stop working because of a storm."

Eric shook his head. "Let's not get carried away just yet. We probably just got turned around in the storm. It'll be fine."

"You saw what Simon and the Siren were capable of." Oliver turned to Eric and locked eyes with him. "The Siren said someone else was pulling the strings—

that Simon had made a deal for a new life in return for Asher's blood."

"I admit what happened a few weeks ago was strange, but—"

"They are coming for him, and I'm sure Mitch won't be the last to die if we don't do something. You saw it yourself. We're trapped here."

Eric looked down at the steering wheel and ran his fingers along its bottom edge. "Better be getting back to town, then." He looked at Oliver and nodded swiftly before putting the car into drive.

The second floor of the pub had fallen in on itself, reducing the building to a few twisted outer walls and a smoldering interior. Several idle stragglers still stood, watching in disbelief. As the station wagon rolled by, they turned and followed the car, realizing who was inside.

A small cluster of cars had been parked next to the town hall.

"We can't leave him like this for everyone to see," Eric said. "Let's take him back to the police station. I know it's a lot to ask, but will you help me carry him in?"

Oliver nodded. "Whatever you need."

Eric pulled around behind the station and backed up to the rear door.

He removed his overcoat and draped it over the

body. "I'll pull him out by his shoulders, and you grab his feet."

Eric walked around to the back and leaned against the car. "Here we go," he said under his breath before opening the door and sliding Mitch to the edge of the seat. Oliver lifted the man by his ankles, and the two carried him inside. The soles of Mitch's shoes had melted, and blistered skin showed through a hole in the bottom.

They took the body to the interrogation room, which had become more of a storage room because of the infrequent nature of Christchurch crime, and set him down carefully on the interview table.

Eric pulled the blinds. "I hate to leave him here, but we don't have much choice at the moment."

They stood over Mitch in an impromptu moment of silence.

"I told her to go to the pub," Oliver said.

"What?"

"I lied about Asher and told the woman she might have better luck at the pub, that he might be staying there. It's my fault. Mitch is dead because of me."

The realization sent another wave of nausea rushing through him, and he searched frantically for a trashcan. He dumped the contents of a paper-recycling basket onto the floor and retched violently into the plastic bin.

Eric knelt down next to him. "It's not your fault."

"I should have helped her. She's probably dead too."

"And what were you going to do? They could have burned the bakery. It could have been you, Anna, and Izzy."

The thought made Oliver want to heave once more.

"Come on," Eric said. "There are paper towels in the bathroom. Go clean yourself up."

CHAPTER FOUR

Oliver opened the doors of the town hall, and the occupants braced themselves against the cold blast that rushed through the building. Most of the town had gathered there, anxiously chattering about the afternoon's events. He stepped over to speak with the mayor, who stood off to the side, talking to one of the Christchurch officers.

Izzy was sitting and sipping coffee out of a Styrofoam cup. When she saw Oliver standing in the doorway, she rushed over as the rest of the crowd took notice.

"You're back so soon," she said. Her eyes seemed to ask what her lips refused to say.

"He didn't make it," he replied. "We tried the road to Amberley, but we're snowed in. We kept getting turned around, like some force didn't want us to leave."

Tears welled in Izzy's eyes. "Oh no, I can't believe it." She wrapped her arthritic hand around Oliver's waist and drew him in for a hug.

The others in the hall noticed the commotion and moved closer to hear.

"We tried our best," Oliver said. "The town must be surrounded by some magic force field, just as Briarwood had been. As soon as we hit the main road to Amberley, the storm got worse, and before we knew it, we were facing the town again."

"But how?" Izzy asked.

"I don't know. But between the Siren's warning and the woman this afternoon, I think we'd better check on Asher and Anna."

Izzy cupped a hand over her mouth. "And we were going to leave him all by himself. How stupid." A serious look crossed her face. "What about the other man?"

"Man?" Oliver asked.

"After you left, they found a man around the side of the building. He managed to crawl out. His arm and the side of his face were burned pretty badly. He said he thought it might have been a gas leak. Gary just left to take him over to the police station. I'm surprised you didn't run into him on the way. He was going to drive the guy over to Amberley."

"But no girl? And they just believed his story?"

"Oliver, he was toast. There's no way he's trying to hurt anyone. Why would he have done that to himself?"

Eric rushed toward the door at the back of the hall, and Oliver chased after him.

His face was still numb from the cold, but the fresh blast of frozen air felt like thousands of tiny needles on his cheeks. He looked around the corner and saw Eric kneeling next to Gary, who was slumped against a wall.

Eric pressed his palm against the officer's stomach. "He's been stabbed," he said. "Come here."

Oliver knelt next to him, and Eric showed him where to apply pressure.

"Put a hand here and press as hard as you can."

Eric went inside for help while Oliver pressed firmly on the man's stomach, trying to staunch the flow of blood.

"Got myself into a mess," Gary said. "Should have never gone alone."

"It's not your fault," Oliver replied.

"I told him." Gary winced.

"Told him what?" Oliver asked.

"About Asher. The guy's face was burned to hell, and I felt bad for him. He said he'd been looking for Asher and wanted to know where he'd been staying. He said he had an urgent message for him."

"What did you tell him?" Oliver felt queasy again.

"That he'd been staying with you and Izzy."

Oliver felt as though the wind had been knocked out of him. "Did you tell him where we live?"

"No. Didn't have time," Gary replied.

"What was the message?"

"Said he'd deliver it himself, then the bastard stabbed me."

Oliver turned toward Izzy's house in the distance, but the snowy haze obscured his view.

"Which way did he go?" Oliver asked.

"I don't know. Was preoccupied with being stabbed and all." His smile turned into another wince. "I'll be okay. Just got me in the fleshy part."

Eric returned with several other townspeople. "Let's get him inside."

"About time," Gary replied. "My ass is numb."

"The man knows Asher is staying with us. We have to go check on him," Oliver told Eric.

"Once we get Gary inside, Will can go with you over to the house."

They guided Gary through the door, helped him to the floor, and leaned him against a wall. A few of the Elders swooped in to tend to his wounds.

Izzy grimaced as she looked at the back seat, still covered with splotches of ash and oxidized blood. She turned away from the car and leaned against it.

"Here," Oliver said. "I'll cover it up." He grabbed a

towel from the trunk and draped it over the dirty leather.

As they drove around the bend to Izzy's house, Oliver held his breath because the car smelled of a grotesque campfire.

Nekko lay in the front bay window as the car pulled up the driveway. As soon as Oliver stopped the car, he opened the door and rushed toward the side entrance.

"Hold on!" Will shouted from behind. "Let me go in first."

He drew his weapon from its holster and twisted the doorknob.

They didn't even bother to lock the door.

Music was blaring from the kitchen as Will entered the back of the house and walked down the hallway toward the sound. He held his hand back, signaling Oliver to stay behind.

When he disappeared around the corner, a sudden shout caused Oliver's heart to jump. He ran down the hall and into the kitchen.

"Startled him," Anna said, bat raised in the air and ready to swing.

Spinach covered the kitchen counters and most of the floor in front of the refrigerator.

"Just making dinner," Asher said as he knelt to gather the leafy greens from the floor. "Nearly gave me a heart attack."

"She's lucky I didn't shoot her," Will said, reholstering his gun.

"Why wasn't the door locked?" Oliver asked.

"Oh," Asher replied. "Must have forgotten to lock it when I took Pan out earlier. You didn't mention that I'd have to worry about rogue police officers sneaking in."

"Seriously?" Anna asked. "The door's been unlocked the whole time?" She leaned the bat against the kitchen table.

"Sorry," Asher added. "It was an honest mistake."

Izzy and Anna crept around the corner.

"Everything all right?" Izzy asked. "I heard shouting from the car."

"Everything's fine," Will replied. "Looks like everything's under control here. Mind giving me a lift back to the square?"

"Should we all go?" Izzy asked.

"There's really not much to do at this point. Lock your doors, and we'll update everyone if there are any developments."

"And how do we reach you if we need help?" she asked.

"Don't think there's a good way at the moment, unfortunately. I'll try to make the rounds now and then. Just have to go back and unbury my cruiser."

"I'll give you a ride." Oliver turned toward the trio standing in the kitchen. "Please, lock the doors this time."

Oliver pulled the car down the driveway and steered toward town. "How are we going to get out of this?" He was asking himself more than Will.

"We just have to find the guy. Couldn't have gotten far with those burns. The man had to have been in agony."

"What about the radios? The phones? We have no way to get help," Oliver said.

"It's just a storm—it will pass," Will replied. "And it's one man against the entire town."

"I'm not so sure about that."

Oliver traced the hillside, looking for the mystery man, but saw nothing more than a blanket of white.

He dropped Will at the police station and helped him dig out one of the police cruisers. The Christchurch police force did most of their work on foot since the town was so small, and all three officers lived within walking distance of the police station.

"Think you might hire more officers, with all that's happened recently?" Oliver asked while scooping snow out from under one of the cruiser's wheels.

"With the way today's gone, we may want to focus on building a fire station first," he replied.

* * *

IZZY LIT a stack of kindling in the living-room fire-place, while Oliver checked all the doors and windows in the house, flipping the lights on as he went.

"Is that necessary?" Izzy asked. "Pretty sure light won't keep the wolves at bay, and it's an awful waste of energy."

"At least we'll be able to see him coming if he does," Oliver replied. "With Gary out of commission, there are only two officers left to protect the entire town, and we have no way to get a hold of them. We're sitting ducks, so we might as well waste a few kilowatts if it gives us a fighting chance."

Izzy waved a hand dismissively.

Anna tapped the bat on the living-room floor. "Let them try to break in. At least one of us will be ready."

Izzy, Anna, Oliver, Asher, Nekko, and Pan all sat in the living room together. Something about the fire made Oliver feel safe. He knew the flames offered no true protection but let himself live the fantasy for a moment.

Wind howled over the hillside as darkness fell on Christchurch.

A knock at the door startled them all. At first, they waited, hoping the person on the other side would go away, but the knocking persisted. Oliver crept to the window as Anna grabbed her bat.

As he peered through the curtains, Eric shouted, "It's me! Let me in." He was standing on the mat, brushing snow from his overcoat and kicking his shoes clean.

"Come in," Oliver said, holding the door open. "We just made coffee."

Eric appeared to be too revved up to sit, and the firelight cast a shifting glow on his face, exaggerating his tired expression and droopy eyes.

"We don't have the resources to look thoroughly, but we haven't found the girl. If she was inside—well, the place is a total loss."

"How's Gary?" Oliver asked.

"Doing okay. I think he'll be fine, but he lost a decent amount of blood. He's going to be weak for the next few days, but at least we'll be able to take care of him without a hospital. Could have been much worse, and I've been driving around all evening but haven't seen the man."

"Have you checked the train station?" Oliver asked. "The woman said she'd taken a train in, and that old train is probably still parked there."

"It is, but the thing is locked tight, and the station is empty."

"So what do we do? Just sit here and wait for him to show up at our door?" Oliver asked.

"I'll be making the rounds this evening." He pulled what appeared to be a bright-orange toy pistol from his pocket. "Since the phones and radio are down, there's no good way to call for help, but if you run into any trouble, just fire this from the window. Will or I should see it."

"A flare gun?" Anna asked.

"You're kidding, right?" Oliver asked.

Eric's expression soured. "Look, a flare is the best we've got for now, unless you want to learn to use smoke signals, and I don't have time for that."

Oliver took the gun from Eric.

"Just click the hammer back and pull the trigger," he said.

"What if the man breaks in?" Izzy asked.

"I have a gun," Oliver replied.

"What? That silly little sword that shoots bullets?" Anna replied.

"It's better than nothing," Eric said.

Oliver cocked his head at Anna. "Better than Izzy's bat, at least."

"My bat saved our keisters last year, if I recall correctly," Izzy said.

Eric chuckled. "Just stay inside and use the flare. I

won't be far away, and if I find anything, I'll let you know."

"How?" Anna asked.

"I'll be back," he replied.

Oliver let Eric out the front door then locked it behind him. "I'll be upstairs if anyone needs me. Who wants the first round of flare duties?" he asked, holding up the orange plastic gun.

Izzy shot a hand up in the air.

"We have one cartridge, so no practice rounds," he said.

Izzy smiled. "I wouldn't think of it."

He handed the flare gun to her and headed to the third floor.

Although he'd buried the weapon at the bottom of his closet, hoping that covering it with old shoe boxes and clothes would somehow reduce the chances he'd ever need it again, he still felt the sword like a heartbeat —much like Poe's story of the tell-tale heart. The guilt he felt for Mercy's death and for leaving Gideon and Briarwood behind was so strong that it seemed to shake the floorboards some nights.

He pulled his dirty-clothes hamper out of the way and tossed a few shoeboxes aside. He'd kept the oblong object bundled in a cloth, which he peeled away carefully.

The sight of the weapon caused his stomach to go

queasy. The last time he'd fired the gun sword was at Simon the year before, and his aim would have only gotten worse without practice. *Does it even still work?* He turned the weapon over in his hands, tracing his fingers along the intricate filigree running up the sword's handle. The leather ammo belt still held more bullets than he would ever need—he hoped. He ensured the chambers were filled with unspent bullets and pulled back both hilt hammers, one by one, just to be sure they hadn't rusted in place.

He tore a piece of paper from his sketch pad and ran the blade of the sword across it, slicing the sheet in half with ease.

Still sharp.

CHAPTER FIVE

A tinny echo crept through the town square and over the hill, reverberating off Izzy's living-room window.

"Did you hear that?" Anna asked as she stuck her fingers through the blinds and peeked out at the front yard.

"Yeah, but what was it?" Oliver opened the front door and stuck his head out while trying to keep his body safe from the cold.

As the sound came again, he held his breath to listen.

"Oliver Crum to the train station." The voice sounded as though it was coming from a megaphone.

"No way." He stepped outside onto the front porch.

The voice returned. "Oliver Crum, please report to the train station."

He turned toward Anna, who gave him a grim look through the crack in the door. "Come back inside," she said. "You'll freeze out there."

Izzy and Asher stood next to her, their arms crossed, bracing themselves from the chill.

"Think it's the man who started the fire?" Anna asked.

"Who else would it be?" Oliver replied.

"I guess we'll never know since you can't go, obviously," Izzy added.

Oliver thought for a moment. "The guy knows Asher's staying with us—the officer told him so. It's only a matter of time before he figures out where we live. Better I go to him than for him to come knocking on our door." He looked across the room at his weapon, sitting on the table. "Maybe I can put an end to this before the situation gets even more out of control." He wasn't sure where this sudden bravado was coming from.

"You can't go out there. You don't know what's waiting for you. And what are you going to do, kill the guy?" Anna stepped toward him. "What if you're walking into a trap? We'll be better off sticking together —four against one."

Oliver wrapped the leather ammo belt around his

waist, tightened it, then zipped his coat, ensuring the weapon was hidden under the puffy material. "I don't know. We'll have even better odds if we know what we're dealing with before he comes knocking on our door. Maybe I can figure out how he's controlling the weather. For all we know, he's just a guy with a box of matches."

He stepped through the door before the others had a chance to talk him out of it. He trudged to the side of the house through the snow, but before he could climb into the station wagon, Anna chased after him, bundled up and clinging tightly to her baseball bat.

"What the hell has gotten into you?" she asked, pointing the bat his direction. "Storming off like that..." She put a hand on the driver's-side door and refused to let him open it.

"I'm sorry," he replied, looking down at the snow.

"This isn't how we do things. We're a family, Oliver."

"You didn't see Mitch gasping for air in the back of Izzy's car. The guy was in agony. To think of something like that happening to you three, or anyone—I can't live with it. Look, I promise... we'll be in this together, but stay here with them, and let me figure out what's happening up there first. I'm sure Eric and Will are already at the train station. They'll have my back."

Anna thought for a moment then backed away

from the door. "All right, but be careful." She leaned the bat against the car and hugged him. "But leave your loner attitude at the train station. We are in this together." She hugged him then opened the car door for him to climb inside.

He made the solitary drive to the train station, passing the remnants of The Horseman. Snow covered the rubble, cooling the hot spots and coating the black layers of ash with a frosting of glittery white.

He set his sights on the train station, hoping he wasn't being foolish for giving the man exactly what he wanted. But he had a weapon strapped to his belt, and taking a chance at the station alone was better than putting Izzy, Asher, and Anna in harm's way.

As he approached, red and blue police lights flashed in the distance.

And I still have two perfectly capable police officers on my side, he thought, trying to reassure himself.

The cruiser sat in the middle of the station entrance, and Eric and Will stood in the crooks of its doors, guns drawn and pointing at an open entrance on the side of the engine of the sleek black locomotive.

"I think it's me they're looking for," Oliver said with a forced grin.

"Just stay back for a minute," Eric shouted over the howling wind.

A brown dress shoe appeared through the door and

lingered for a moment as if testing the waters for itchy trigger fingers.

"Come out now!" Eric yelled.

A man emerged, the leg of his navy-blue pinstripe suit flapping in the wind as he stepped out onto the metal step of the train door. He gripped an old-style microphone, attached to a cord inside the train, and held his fedora to keep it from flying away in the violent wind, obscuring a patch of slicked-back red hair.

"Now, judging by the looks of it, you must be Oliver." He pointed in Oliver's direction.

The microphone fed into a set of speakers on top of the train that reminded Oliver of the large tornado sirens perched on his elementary school.

"Doesn't matter who he is!" Eric shouted. "Put the microphone down and walk slowly toward us."

"Oh, I don't think so," the man replied. "We've got so much to do and so little time." He chuckled. "Speaking of time... It's time for you to climb aboard." He gestured to Oliver.

Oliver took a step out into the snow toward the train.

"No!" Eric shouted. "Stay where you are."

"Relax," the man said through the loudspeaker. "Just need a few moments with the boy. I assure you I will return him in one piece... unless he does something stupid." His laugh was high pitched and rapid-fire, like a hyena's.

"It's fine," Oliver said. "I'm not the one he really wants anyway."

"Ooh, it's like you read the last chapter before the first. Don't go spoiling it for the rest of them," the man said.

Oliver stepped toward the train, but Eric approached from behind and grabbed his arm.

"Let go," Oliver said as he wrenched free. "I'll be fine."

When Oliver reached the train's doorway, the man motioned for Oliver to stop. "Take off your coat."

Oliver hesitated.

"What? You thought I'd let you onto the train without checking for weapons? This isn't my first day on the job. Take off your coat."

Oliver unzipped his coat, revealing the odd-looking sword underneath.

The man laughed. "Leave it with your jacket."

Oliver reluctantly removed the ammo belt and tossed both his coat and belt into the snow. He held his hands in the air to show he wasn't holding any other weapons.

The man stepped aside for him. As he mounted the first metal step, a blast of warm air radiated from the doorway. He climbed into the engine and looked back, hoping he hadn't just made a stupid decision.

As he entered, Oliver noticed the engine didn't look like an engine at all. Deep cherry hardwood lined the floor, and blackout curtains covered the windows, providing space for a row of bookshelves and display cases.

If not for the dire situation, Oliver would have taken more time to admire the intricate trinkets lining its walls. Still, he wondered how everything stayed in place, considering the entire display was sitting on a train.

"Like my collection?" The man climbed up behind Oliver and hit a button on the wall, which caused the heavy metal door to slide into place. "Was getting chilly out there," he said, rubbing his hands together.

Oliver clenched his fists. "Just tell me who you are and what you want so I can be on my way."

"Kitty's got claws," he replied, curling his fingers and hissing as Nekko did when Pan got on her nerves. He cackled once more, his head twitching slightly.

Oliver thought of Mitch's charred body lying limp on the police station's interrogation table and the woman who likely lay buried somewhere in the rubble.

"You're a murderer," Oliver said through gritted teeth.

The man feigned offense and pressed his hands to

his chest. "I've murdered no one—you can blame the flame for that," the man said, turning toward a serving cart in one corner of the room. "I'm shocked you came. Thought I would have to hunt you down. It's very brave of you. Bourbon?"

"No," Oliver replied.

The man tonged a large ice cube from an ice bucket.

"To be fair, Mitch might have made it, had you not driven off the road." He dropped the first cube into a glass tumbler and giggled.

Oliver's blood boiled, and his fingers itched for his weapon. If only he hadn't left it in the snow...

"And the officer—well, that's just poor police training. What kind of podunk town has three police officers and no hospital?" He dropped a second cube into his glass and poured from a decanter. "He should be fine, though. Think I missed the vital organs. The man's suffered enough, living in this hellhole."

"But why? Why kill someone?"

"Who? Mitch? Copped a bit of a 'tude when I asked about Asher. Didn't like his style, so thought burning down his bar might teach him a lesson." He slurped loudly from the tumbler. "Thought the poor guy could move faster, though. Pity." He snickered.

"You're a monster," Oliver said.

"No, no." The man set his glass on the table. "A

monster would turn away a woman in need of help in a snowstorm." He pulled a metal lighter from his pocket and flicked the wheel with his thumb, sending bursts of sparks into the air.

The man was an odd assemblage of tics and gestures and stood a solid foot shorter than Oliver. *Hardly a super villain.*

"And look where we are now," the man drew closer, "in the same place we would have been had you told the truth. Except now, one person is dead, and the other is bleeding like a stuck pig. So think more carefully before slinging words like 'monster' around so freely. And you haven't even seen a real monster." The man was spitting as he spoke, and his head twitched back and forth with the beats of his speech.

At first, Oliver looked for a blunt object with which to defend himself, but he swallowed his fear and stepped toward the man, staring down into his beady black eyes. "Where is the girl? Kill her too?"

The man's angry expression faded. "Kill her? I wish I could kill the bitch. No, she's very much alive. Too important, unfortunately."

"What do you mean, 'too important'?"

"That's neither here nor there. Come with me to the office." He picked up his glass from the bar and walked toward the door at the far end of the engine.

He led Oliver to the passenger car. The sound of

flowing water caught him by surprise. A fish tank ran alongside each wall, filled to the brim with tropical fish and coral.

"I'm a bit of a collector, in case you haven't noticed," the man said. "Books, antiques, fish, trains— now people." He laughed again as he took a seat at an intricately carved wooden desk at the back of the room, sliding a stack of notebooks out of the way and shoving them into a desk drawer. "In fact, you can call me the Collector if you'd like. It's got a nice ring to it."

"What's your real name?" Oliver asked.

"Never had the luxury of a name of my own." The Collector gestured for Oliver to take a seat.

"I'll stand," Oliver replied. "Just tell me what you want."

"Down to business, I see," he replied. The man furrowed his brow. "I think you know perfectly well what I came for."

"You can't have him."

"I assure you I'm taking nothing I'm not owed. Since Simon couldn't follow up on his end of our bargain, I came to claim my fee and be on my way. Bring Asher to me, and your town will be back to normal within the hour." He leaned back in his chair and gave Oliver a sly smile. "Sound reasonable?"

Oliver stepped toward the man and leaned over the desk. "Asher isn't an object to be collected. He's not just something that can be passed from one person to another."

"Did you see the displays on the way in?"

"What do they have to do with anything?"

"Cabinets full of priceless artifacts, shelves lined with first editions, and tropical aquariums with some of the rarest fish even zoos can't get a hold of." He waved his hand at the tanks across the room.

"Why are you telling me this?" Oliver asked.

"I'm accustomed to getting what I want. I'm very good at it, in fact. This train, for example. Saw it in a magazine when I was younger. Always dreamt of owning one myself. I ran into the owner of one a few years ago. Then I ran into him again and again until he was no longer in a state to own a train of such beauty. So I took it off his hands. I think the man still had hands by the time I was done with him. I made a few modifications. He'd kept it in terrible condition."

Oliver sat across from the man and folded his arms on the desk. "The last guy who came here for Asher ended up dead in a field. You don't scare me."

That last bit was a lie, and the only reason Oliver's hands weren't visibly shaking was because he had clasped them tightly together.

"I didn't scare the bartender or that pig either." The man held an index finger to his lips and grinned. "I like you," he said, leaning back in his chair and flipping his lighter around in his hands. "You're like one of those dolls that says heroic catchphrases every time you pull its string."

He looked at his watch. "Let's see—nine o'clock now. I'll give you until dawn to bring Asher to the train. If he's not here by sunrise, I will come looking for him and will be sure to burn to the ground anyone and anything that gets in my way." He clicked the flint wheel, and a flame rose from the tip of the lighter. "I have a proclivity for fire, so try not to test me on this one."

"Don't you have enough of his blood already? With the stolen tank from The Parlor and the specimen jars —what more could you need?"

The man leaned in. "That's just enough to get me started. Simon didn't understand the boy's true power. He may have lit a few torches and healed a few wounds, but Asher's blood is more than that—it's cosmic fuel. I will have him."

"Awful trusting to assume we won't leave town," Oliver replied.

"You and I both know that's not possible. Nothing comes in, and nothing goes out. Until I have Asher, winter will continue in Christchurch."

Oliver sat back in the chair. "How are you doing it? Are you an Unnatural?"

"You're wasting valuable time with all these questions. But I tell you what." He opened one of the desk drawers, pulled out a thick stack of hundred-dollar bills, and tossed them on the table.

"Because I like you, I'll sweeten the pot. Consider this a finder's fee. It's yours if you bring him here. You have till sunrise to think about it before I come knocking. And I knock hard. Would be a shame too—it's a beautiful home."

Oliver's eyes widened.

"What?" he asked. "You think I wasn't watching? I saw the car come from over the hill on the outskirts of town. Few houses out that way, from what I've seen." He grinned.

"You will never have him," Oliver said as he pounded a fist on the desk.

The man rolled his eyes. "And what will you say if I pull the string again? Please don't waste my time with your pathetic macho-man act. I have to say I'm offended you're not more receptive to my generosity. I could have mowed this town over, and no one would have noticed. Instead, I offer you money, and you insult me with the pathetic excuse for a weapon that's rusting out in the snow." The man stood and led Oliver to the doorway. "Now, let me show you the door so you can go mull over my proposition although there isn't much to consider. Bring me the boy, or I burn your town to the ground." He cocked his head to one side and smiled.

Oliver turned to reply, but before he could, the man pressed the button on the wall, and the metal door in the side of the room shot open. With a swift kick, he knocked Oliver out of the train car into the deep snow. He turned to look back, but the metal door had shot back into place, leaving no access to the iron fortress.

Eric rushed to his side, while Will tried with no luck to pry the door open.

"Are you all right?" Eric asked.

"Fine," Oliver replied as he stood up and brushed himself off. He bent down to pick up his weapon and coat and wiped off the shiny metal.

"What did he say?"

"He said I have until sunrise to bring Asher to the train."

"But why?"

"Asher's blood. He says it's 'cosmic fuel.'"

"Oliver... you don't really believe—"

"You saw it for yourself!" Oliver snapped. "You aren't allowed to be a skeptic, Eric. *You* nearly shot me, point blank, last year because I broke a damned violin. *You* know there's something going on here you can't explain away with reason, so cut the crap. This train won't leave here without Asher, and he's threatened to destroy anyone and anything that gets in the way. So you can either help me or stay the hell out of my way."

Eric took a step back. "Look, I know there's something going on that I don't quite get, but we're trying to help, trying to keep the town safe when there's just the two of us. But you've got to give me a minute, and you can't go flying off the handle and expect things to work out in your favor."

Oliver shook his head. "What are we going to do, then?"

"You're going back to Izzy's," Eric replied. "The guy might have an edge on us while he's locked up in that train, but he can't drive it across the square. He'll have to come out, and when he does, we'll be waiting."

"And what am I supposed to do?" Oliver asked. "Sit and wait for him to knock on the door?"

"If he can get through us and comes knocking on your door, we've got bigger problems to worry about," Eric replied.

CHAPTER SIX

Oliver lay in bed, watching snowflakes fall outside as Nekko's head rested on his breastbone, her soft purr vibrating through his chest. Typically, he'd have pushed the cat off his stomach hours before, but her presence comforted him. He ran his hands through her fur, thoughts of what awaited him at sunrise racing through his head.

He'd spent many sleepless nights in his third-floor bedroom, worried about the Witch, worried about the Siren, even worried about his mother. Now, he found himself sleepless again, wondering whether tomorrow would tear his newfound family apart and whether tonight might very well be his last sleepless night at Izzy's... or his last night period.

Eric and Will had planted themselves firmly between the train station and the town, hoping to protect it from the man who'd called himself the Collector. He was just a man, or so Oliver thought. Still, as the mysterious storm raged, Oliver wondered how the Collector was controlling the blizzard and just what other secret weapons he held behind the steel walls of the sleek locomotive.

After several hours of tossing and turning, Oliver abandoned sleep completely and rolled out of bed toward the window. The snowfall had let up momentarily, and although the sky was still dark, the snow-covered ground reflected the moon's rays, casting a glow in the atmosphere.

Christchurch appeared sleepy and peaceful in the distance, but he wondered how many other towns-people lay awake that evening, Mitch's death fresh in their minds.

He shook his head and tried to clear it of all the panicked thoughts racing through. The floorboards creaked as he crossed the landing to Asher's room. He stuck his head inside, but Asher's bed was empty. *So I'm not the only one who can't sleep.*

As he reached the second floor, he heard chatter from the first and climbed downstairs, holding his weapon and ammo belt in one hand and gripping the railing with the other. When he reached the kitchen, Asher, Anna, and Izzy were all sitting around the table as though they'd been there for some time.

They'd all resolved to stay in the house, where the four of them would face the man together if he came knocking. If Eric and Will couldn't stop him, they would be ready.

"None of you could sleep either?" he asked.

Someone had gathered a collection of weapons from around the house. Several bats and a hockey stick leaned against the kitchen table, a blunt object for each of them.

"Don't you think that might be overkill?" Oliver asked, nodding at the cache.

"I'd rather be over-prepared than caught by surprise," Izzy replied. "I learned that during my protest days. Coffee? Was just about to put another pot on."

"Sounds great," he replied.

Izzy hopped up from the table and walked over to the coffeepot.

Oliver set his weapon down and took a seat. "I got tired of lying in bed. How long have you all been up?"

"An hour or so," Asher replied. "I nodded off once or twice, just long enough to have a few horrifying nightmares."

Izzy returned, set a coffee cup in front of Oliver, and filled it with the rest of the coffee from the pot before turning the machine on to brew a fresh one.

"I hate sitting here, just waiting for something to

happen. I feel so helpless," Izzy said as she returned to the table.

"I know," Oliver replied. "I'm sure they'll grab him as soon as he comes out of the train. He can't stay locked away in there *and* come after us, can he? And if he does, we have our own weapons." Oliver patted the handle of his gun sword.

"Let's just hope he doesn't have something more modern, like—I don't know—a revolver." Anna smirked.

"Hey, it's better than that bat you've been carrying around," he shot back.

Anna stuck her tongue out.

"I wish I could figure out how he's keeping us locked in. I don't think he's doing it himself. Think he's got another Unnatural onboard?" Oliver sipped his coffee cautiously but still burned his lips. "I asked him if he was an Unnatural, and he waffled. And if he was the same burned man they found near the pub, I didn't see any burns."

"Let's just hope that Eric can get onboard and find out," Anna replied.

"And the woman. I thought he'd killed her, but he said she was still alive. I wonder if she could be controlling the storm." Oliver pressed his head into his hands and massaged his temples. "Why can't we just have a normal fall: an ordinary old Halloween with *fake* witches and a Thanksgiving where no one's burned to death? Is it too much to ask? Hasn't this town been through enough?" He looked up at the others.

"I don't know what *normal* is anymore." Anna grinned.

Oliver shook his head. "We'll get through this, right?" He wanted to be strong, but the question had been percolating in his head, and the severity of the situation brought it spilling out.

"All we can do is try," Izzy replied, "and our track record has been good so far."

"You're right," he replied, looking up from the table. "Let him come."

By dawn, the crew sitting at Izzy's kitchen table had consumed several pots of coffee and force-fed themselves breakfast. Orange slivers of morning light moved along the walls as sun rays sneaked through the breaks in the clouds. Oliver stepped to the back of the kitchen to peer out the window. The scene outside was deceptively peaceful. The sunlight was a reminder that a world still existed outside Christchurch's invisible walls.

"Wonder how long it'll take the guy to figure out we're not coming," he asked.

Asher rubbed his forehead. "I don't know, but I wish he'd get on with it. I'm too wired and stressed to sleep but too tired to do much of anything else."

A frantic knock made them all jump, and Pan ran through the living room, yapping loudly.

Oliver lifted his weapon from the table and clicked one of the hammers.

"He couldn't have gotten through. The police were guarding the train." Anna reached for her bat, her eyes wide with concern.

"I don't know," he replied, holding his fingers to his lips. "I'll go see who it is."

Another violent pounding echoed through the house.

Oliver approached the front door, training the barrel of his weapon at its center.

"Who is it?" he shouted.

"It's Eric. For God's sake, let me in!" Oliver hadn't heard that level of desperation in Eric's voice since he'd pleaded for the sound of the Siren's violin.

He lowered his weapon and approached the door. As soon as he flipped the lock, Eric rushed inside and slammed the door behind himself. As Pan leapt at his legs, he bent over and tried to catch his breath.

"What happened?" Oliver asked as the others emerged from the doorway into the living room.

"Go, now," he said. "You've got maybe five minutes before he gets here. He'll burn the place to the ground —make sure you take everyone. Get as far away from town as you can. We'll come find you once it's safe."

"But how? He's just got a lighter," Oliver replied.

Eric let out a nervous laugh. "That's what I thought. It's more than that. The flames come from his hands."

"We can go to the cottage," Anna said.

"No, he'll go door-to-door until he finds you. You have to leave town," Eric replied.

Oliver was dumbfounded. "What are you going to do? Come with us."

"No, I've got to stay here and help the others. Take care of yourself," he said. "Just go! I'll try to hold him off." He turned toward the front door and was gone before Oliver could process what had just happened.

As Eric trudged back to his car, Oliver caught a glimpse of smoke rolling from the far side of the square.

He turned toward the others, whose faces were terror stricken.

"Where do we go?" Anna asked.

"I don't know," Oliver replied.

"We have to go back, don't we?" Asher asked, stepping toward the window to look outside.

"Back?" Anna asked.

"Back to Briarwood."

"Are you sure it's safe?" Izzy asked.

"Gideon's alive," Oliver replied. "I've seen him at the edge of the woods. He might be able to help us."

"You saw him?" Izzy asked. "Why didn't—"

"I think we should do it," Asher said, as if trying to get the words out before good sense persuaded him otherwise. He turned toward them. "If you think Gideon will help us, I'd be willing to take the risk. We'll be harder to find there, anyway."

"Are you sure?" Oliver asked. "I'm far from certain."

Asher shrugged. "We don't have much time to debate. We've got to go now, and I think Briarwood is the best option."

Oliver nodded. "Let's get going, then."

They pulled their coats and boots from the hall closet and bundled up as best they could.

Asher stood at the back window, his face as pale as the snow accumulating outside.

"You look like you're going to be sick," Oliver said.

Asher swallowed hard. "What if it doesn't work? What will stop him from waltzing right into Briarwood? Don't exactly need this to get in anymore." From under his shirt, he pulled the chain holding the Briarwood key.

"We'll find Gideon, and he'll help us. This guy doesn't have a chance." Oliver tried to sound confident but wasn't sure he'd convinced Asher.

Asher turned toward him. "I could walk right over to the train station, and things would be back to normal by tomorrow. Just promise you'll let me go if the Briar-wood plan fails."

"That really what you want to do?" Oliver asked.

"No. I just don't want anyone else to suffer to save me."

Oliver thought back to his conversation with Anna, when she chased him as he left for the train station. "We'll figure this out, and we'll do it together."

"Just promise me, if it comes down to it, you'll let me go."

"I promise." Oliver rolled his eyes.

"Who's taking the cat?" Izzy asked as she entered the kitchen, carrying Pan and wearing an old leather belt with a baseball bat looped through it.

The pets...

"We can't leave them," she said. "You saw what happened to the bar."

"You're right," he said.

"I'll grab the cat!" Asher shouted from the living room.

The early winter wind cut through Oliver's jeans as he pulled his coat tight around himself, and the snow clung to them as they traversed the hill as quickly as their feet could carry them. Nekko, happy to let someone do the walking for her, burrowed herself in Asher's arms and nuzzled against his chest, trying to absorb his body heat. Pan squirmed in Izzy's grip, whining desperately to be put down.

The scene must have looked absurd—a train of people trudging down a snowy hill with a fat cat and a corgi.

Although Oliver kept a steady pace, Asher was gradually slowing.

"Doing all right back there?" he asked.

"Just preparing myself," Asher replied.

"They won't even recognize you. You weren't exactly in the best shape, considering you were covered in blood and all."

They came to the edge of the briars, or at least where the briars had once been. Snow had covered most of the broken brambles, but several dead branches stuck out.

"They're harmless now," Oliver said, stepping into the crunchy patch. He wasn't sure exactly where the invisible dome had been, but that mattered little ever since it had come crashing to the ground.

As they approached the ruins of the stone house at the edge of Briarwood, Oliver kept a close eye on the trees in front of him.

Oliver recognized the foundation of the collapsed building Asher had shown him a few weeks before. Although the ruins were covered with snow, scorch marks still showed on the far wall—the only wall still standing. A thick roof beam lay up against the charred stone. The body they'd seen before had been covered, too, and Oliver chose not to mention it to Anna and Izzy.

They passed the broken lampposts that once lit the way into town, powered by the magical blood flowing through Asher's veins.

When they reached the edge of the town square, Oliver stepped out from behind a tree at its border to get a closer look. The shops had all been boarded up, and one had even collapsed in on itself. The toppled statue of Nathaniel Hale had been cleared, leaving an empty pedestal.

The impossibly proportioned town hall sat on the far end of the square. The metal lantern room on the side of the building—the same one from which the Witch had burst a year earlier—still hung broken, copper bracing mangled and clinging desperately to shards of broken glass. The main structure stood strong although the stones had been scorched on one side and debris littered the front steps.

"Maybe this was a mistake," Asher whispered.

"Just a drop," someone said from behind.

Oliver held in a scream and turned around.

"I just needs me a drop, just to quench my thirst."

A man seemed to sway in the wind as if he were a scarecrow held up by a flimsy wooden stake. *Thin* would have been an understatement—he was malnourished, and his skin seemed almost translucent. Oxidized blood caked his body, so much that Oliver had a hard time telling whether he was wearing clothes. In the heavy snow, he must have been freezing but didn't seem to care.

Pan wriggled in Izzy's arms and barked frantically at the blood-soaked man.

"Are you all right?" Oliver asked.

"Just let me have a drop, and I'll be on my way." He twitched.

"We don't have any water," Oliver replied.

"No, no—not water." The man's body convulsed as he let out a sickening cackle.

He pulled a knife from his belt.

"Let me cut your skin, just a little. Just give me a drop."

He took a step forward and lifted the knife.

"Sometimes I can get a bit carried away, though." He laughed again. "It's not my fault. The blood just tastes so good on my lips."

The man stood between them and the woods, preventing them from fleeing back to Christchurch. Oliver fumbled with his zipper, trying to reach for the weapon underneath his coat as he stepped in front of Izzy and Anna.

"At least the loud creature," he said, pointing at

Pan. "Let me have it!" The man screamed as he rushed toward them.

The crack of Anna's bat against the man's shoulder echoed through the square. He stepped back and screamed, grabbing his shoulder as Anna raised her bat again.

Oliver finally freed the gun sword from his coat as the man lunged. But before Oliver could pull the trigger or Anna could swing, the attacker stopped short, grunted, and stepped backward. He gripped an arrow embedded in his chest. As blood flowed down his torso, he didn't seem concerned about pain—rather, he tried to catch his blood before it hit the ground.

"You're letting it out!" he screamed. "I need it!" He began lapping the fluid from his hands. "I need it!" he shouted again before falling into the snow.

Something rustled in the trees on the side of the square, but before Oliver could flee, someone grabbed him from behind. He glimpsed Asher and a hand that covered his mouth as both of them were dragged toward a shop. He tried to pull free, but the lumbering figure towering over him was much too strong.

As soon as they were all inside, one kidnapper slammed the door.

"Gideon," Oliver said, spinning around as soon as the assailant let go of him. Anna cracked the other man in the leg with her bat as soon as she had a clear shot. Arrows spilled from his quiver and fell to the floor.

The archer shouted as he let go of Asher and fell against the wall, gripping his shin.

"It's okay," Oliver said, holding out a hand. "They won't hurt us. Will you?" he asked Gideon.

Gideon stood in front of him, his head wrapped with a bandage covering his left eye. His clothes were ripped and worn, and he looked as though he'd been dragged through the mud. He seemed to debate the question before shaking his head.

"See, you can relax," Oliver said, holding his hand out to prevent Anna from striking again.

"Silence that beast!" the archer shouted at Izzy while he sat on the floor, rubbing his shin.

Pan was still in a frenzy, and Asher scrambled to gather Nekko from the corner of the room. Fortunately, she wasn't difficult to catch.

The storefront, once filled with clothing, sat empty, aside from a few stray garments strewn about, covered in mold and rot.

"What happened here?" Oliver asked.

Shouting came from across the square, and a brigade of boots and breaking branches broke the momentary silence.

"We can't stay. The blood seekers are on our trail," the archer said.

Before Oliver could ask another question, Gideon grabbed him by an arm and led him toward the back door.

"Can't we hide downstairs?" Oliver asked, but Gideon ignored the question. He pulled a mechanical ball from his pocket, pressed a panel in the center, then set it on the floor.

Once outside, Gideon led them behind the Clock-maker's shop and hid behind the trees bordering the square.

"When I say, we run to the corner of the hall. If you fall behind, we will leave you to the blood seekers," the archer said.

Oliver did not understand who the blood seekers were, but he wasn't willing to find out firsthand.

"Understand?" he asked.

Oliver nodded, and the archer turned toward the others, who also agreed.

"And shut him up," he said again to Izzy, who tried to hold Pan's snout closed to prevent him from barking.

A band of men emerged from behind the brush at the corner of the square—three blood-soaked beings who looked no better off than the man who'd been shot with the arrow—each brandishing rusted metal weapons.

As Pan whined, Oliver was sure he'd give them all away until a shrill ringing blasted from Gideon's old clothing shop caught the trio's attention. The man in front screamed a random assemblage of incoherent syllables.

Once they'd gone inside the shop, Gideon pushed Oliver forward.

"Run," the archer whispered before taking off across the square.

They followed Gideon as closely as they could, but Oliver hadn't needed to run for his life in some time and wasn't exactly in running-for-his-life shape.

As they reached the Briarwood town hall, they ran past the front to the side entrance, where Oliver had been taken to the dungeon a year prior.

Gideon pounded on the door, and the viewing panel slid open on the other side, followed by the clunk of a heavy reinforcement bar falling to the floor.

Oliver had flashbacks of his time spent in the dungeon, suffocated by the darkness. Once everyone had shuffled inside and Gideon closed the door behind himself, Oliver recognized the man guarding it. The Clockmaker struggled to lift the heavy bar and brace it across the door, his wispy hair thinner than before and his hunch more pronounced. Gideon leaned in to help him.

"They'll be close behind," the archer said.

The Clockmaker slipped the peephole open once

more then shut it again and locked it in place with a wooden peg.

The dungeon below the town hall had been converted into a workshop of sorts, and Oliver recognized several gadgets from the Clockmaker's shop. A few bulky machines were stationed in one corner of the room, and clusters of metal rods hung over the edges of a set of shelves beside boxes full of assorted gears, screws, and other shiny pieces.

The Clockmaker turned, still mumbling to himself about the sturdiness of the door. When he saw Oliver, he stopped midsentence, straightened his crooked back, and placed a hand atop his head, on the bald spot nestled between two clouds of nebulous gray fluff.

"Well, praise be. Never thought I'd see you again." The Clockmaker approached and placed a hand on Oliver's shoulder. "I'm so glad."

The warm welcome surprised Oliver.

Gideon's eyes were locked on Asher, who stood next to the doorway.

Oliver thought back to the night in Asher's cell below Simon's bedroom. He, Gideon, and Mercy were the only three to see Asher that night. And Gideon seemed to recognize him but didn't give him the welcoming look Oliver had received from the Clockmaker.

The archer noticed Gideon's stare. "What's the matter?" he asked.

Gideon opened his mouth and looked as though he wanted to scream, but as far as Oliver knew, the man was still mute. Gideon rushed across the room, grabbed Asher by the collar, and pressed him into the stone wall.

"Wait!" Oliver shouted and tried to pull Gideon away. "He's with me—with us." But Gideon had already removed a dagger from his belt.

"No!" Asher yelled and lifted his arms to shield his face.

Gideon brought the blade down with a swift flick, nicking the skin on Asher's forearm.

"What are you doing? Stop!" Oliver shouted.

A trickle of blood formed at the corner of the cut, and a phosphorescent drop splattered to the floor.

Gideon jerked Asher around and held his arm for the others to see.

The archer's expression soured. "You're the reason for all of this."

"I haven't done anything," Asher replied.

"What do we do with him?" the archer asked Gideon.

Gideon nodded in the direction of the door to the square.

"If they're after his blood, we'll give it to them." He

walked to the door and began to lift the bar, while Gideon dragged Asher over to the door.

Anna raised her weapon, but before she reached the archer, Oliver aimed the barrel of the gun sword at the man.

"I said stop!" Oliver shouted.

"You still have it," the Clockmaker said in amazement, ignoring the severity of the situation.

"What's your game?" the archer asked. "His blood nearly destroyed this town. Now you have brought him back... for what? To destroy us all? Between the storm and the blood seekers, we don't need your help to achieve that destiny."

"To save his life. To save our town," Oliver replied. "We need your help."

"And why should we help you?" he asked.

"If you want the storm to end, you have no choice."

"And how do you control the sky?"

"Not me, but the man who came looking for Asher. He calls himself the Collector."

"A wanted fellow, eh?" the Clockmaker asked, still oblivious to the tension in the air.

"If you help us, we'll be able to end the storm and get rid of the blood seekers." The name *blood seeker* was self-explanatory, but Oliver wondered who they were and why they wanted to torment the town.

The archer relaxed his grip on the bar and looked at Gideon, who shrugged.

"Fine," the archer replied. "Now please aim your weapon somewhere else."

Oliver lowered the gun and clicked the hammer back into place. "So we have a deal, then?"

"Not so much a deal as a reluctant agreement, perhaps," the archer replied. "I'm Aymes." He extended his hand.

"Good enough," Oliver replied as he lowered his weapon and crossed the room to shake Aymes's hand. "And these are Anna and Izzy."

"Can I see it?" the Clockmaker asked, holding out his withered hands for Oliver to hand him the weapon. "It's been so long."

"Let him go first," Oliver said, glancing at Gideon, who still had a firm grip on Asher.

Gideon loosened his grip, and Asher pulled himself away.

"Here." Oliver flipped the weapon around so that the Clockmaker could grip the handle.

"It's been so long," he said once more. "I made this to fit *her* hands. Always had such big hands. The boys called her 'ogre' when she was a child, at least until she sent a few home with blackened eyes." He felt the weight of the weapon as it rested in his palms. "Just the perfect size for her."

"I'm sorry," Oliver said.

The Clockmaker looked down at his feet then up at Oliver. "You have nothing to be sorry for. She knew what she was getting herself into."

"I'm sorry I didn't come back—that I left you here to fight by yourselves."

"And how would you have helped? Not exactly a soldier, are you?" Aymes asked.

"No, but—"

"The blood seekers would have devoured you. Just be glad there are still people in this town for them to feed on. Once they run out, your town is next."

Oliver felt a chill run up his spine. "You know about the barrier?"

"Know about it? We saw it fall from the sky," Aymes replied.

"Why haven't you fled, then?"

"Too risky. We'd only be trading one danger for another. At least this danger is known."

"Why are they after you? What's wrong with them?" Oliver asked.

Aymes thought for a moment. "Let's take a walk."

CHAPTER SEVEN

Izzy and Anna stayed behind with Gideon while Aymes and the Clockmaker led Oliver and Asher through the town hall. The corridor, once brought to life by odd-colored flames from flickering wall sconces, now sat dark. Aymes pulled a torch from the workshop wall and held it out in front of him, lighting the pathway.

"It wasn't long after we booted that wretched man from power that word spread about the blood. Those who knew of its properties traded the secret for safety and privilege although most met terrible fates at the hands of the blood seekers."

Oliver thought of Elias, Simon's assistant, whom he'd met while locked in the dungeon.

"There seemed to be a limitless supply, at first. We

started using it for treatment, to heal wounds and cure diseases," the Clockmaker said.

They climbed a back staircase and crisscrossed several hallways before reaching the wood-paneled landing that led to the room above the town hall atrium.

"But some started to drink it—not for healing but for pleasure and power. Vials set aside for treatment would go missing, and those who kept control of the blood started to see it as a right, as a prize for having led the town out of darkness. So they drank."

"And you didn't?" Oliver asked.

"No," Aymes replied. "The older men became spry again, and the younger ones built muscle. They brought the blood to their families. They all drank. But the looks in their eyes changed—became vacant as if they stared through the world without truly seeing it."

He pressed a wood panel that shifted out of the way to reveal the staircase to the platform.

"They underestimated how quickly the supply would dwindle," the Clockmaker said as he hobbled behind them.

"The blood brought strength and vigor, but when it left, so did the remaining humanity in those who relied on it," Aymes said. "As their bodies thinned and faded, so did their minds. They became desperate, animalistic. I'm not sure when or how, but one of the blood seekers discovered that those who had consumed the blood still carried a little inside them. Townspeople turned on each other, and fathers turned on their families, killing their wives and children for another taste of blood."

They climbed the stairs to the top of the platform. The room had once been filled with a lavalike glow from the expansive pool of vibrant liquid but now sat dark and desolate.

"The lights extinguished half a year ago when the blood ran out," Aymes said.

"Can I see?" Oliver asked, pointing at the portal that had once protected Simon's private residence.

"Go ahead." Aymes waved him on.

Oliver stepped through the portal of twisted copper scales. He felt a cold breeze through the crack at the bottom of Simon's office door. When he twisted the handle, a gust of winter air greeted him.

"No one has been here for a few months. No use for the place, really," the Clockmaker said.

Snow covered Simon's desk and the surrounding area. Although the back of the room, near the entrance, had been somewhat protected from the elements, the books, once so neatly arranged on the bookshelf, lay strewn about the floor.

"Why did you tear the place apart?" Oliver asked.

Aymes knelt and picked a book from the floor.

"Wasn't us. After the well ran dry, the blood seekers pilfered every drawer, crack, and crevice in search of blood vials. Simon kept them hidden everywhere."

Oliver walked across the room toward Simon's grand desk and the lantern-like chandelier hanging above it. The lantern that had once burned brightly now sat dark and had corroded from exposure to the elements.

Simon's desk drawers had been pulled free and their contents dumped in piles now covered in snow.

Shards of glass still lay scattered at the base of the window where the Witch had burst through, and the heavy door that had once held her was ripped from its hinges. Oliver stood next to Simon's desk and looked out upon the devastated town below.

His eyes traced the landscape to the top of the hill where Izzy's house sat in the distance. Considering Eric's frantic plea for them to flee, Oliver expected to see Christchurch in shambles. Dawn had come and gone, but the sleepy town still sat mostly undisturbed.

As they crossed through the entryway from Simon's office back toward the platform, Asher stopped and turned toward the door to Simon's private quarters.

"I remember this place. It's this way, isn't it? My room?" he asked.

Oliver nodded.

"Go have a look. Won't find much in there—it's been raided for supplies," Aymes added.

Asher timidly turned the knob leading to Simon's dining room and stepped inside.

Once an elegant dining space, the room had been trashed, much like the rest of Simon's compound. The upturned dining table leaned awkwardly against the far wall, and broken plates crunched under their feet.

The Clockmaker pulled a chair from next to the toppled table. "I'll rest here, if that's all right."

Aymes eyed another chair in the corner. "Me too. I've seen his private quarters, and I don't care to see them again."

"Will you come with me?" Asher asked Oliver. "I want to see my old room."

Oliver wondered why Asher would want to see the cell that had held him captive for so long, but he obliged.

They walked through Simon's living area, passing broken furniture and piles of debris until they reached the hallway leading to his bedroom. The bed had been eviscerated, and feathers coated the floor. The blood seekers had left no drawer unsearched nor surface untouched. The bookcase concealing the secret room was ajar, and Asher squeezed through to the spiral staircase on the other side. Oliver followed closely but was careful to give Asher his space. When he reached the bottom of the staircase, Asher was already inside the cell, looking out the small window.

"This window was my portal to the world," he said, "just a sliver of the town square. Everything else came from books." Asher walked across the room to a set of bookcases, careful to avoid the chair where Oliver had first found him bleeding and broken. His books lay in a heap on the floor, and he knelt to flip through them.

"Coming here must stir up a lot of emotions," Oliver said.

"Mostly fear that the townspeople would drag me out into the square and hang me. Relatives of defeated dictators rarely fare well." He reached for an old book on world history, which appeared to be from a library.

Asher traced his fingers along the pages. "Did I ever tell you I saw them topple the statue?"

"No, you didn't."

"Comical would have been the best way to describe it, had it not been for the fact they were trying to overthrow my father—a bunch of men with hammers against a bronze statue. They almost lost the battle."

"I can't imagine."

"Eventually, they had to tie one end of a rope around the statue's neck and the other to a bull. A part of me was looking forward to walking in the fresh air on the way to the gallows. I'd seen people come and go for years across that square, and I was always curious what it would be like to walk it myself."

"If you saw the statue, you must have seen me after they tied me to the base."

"I did, but I have to admit I was more focused on my sister and how awful she looked. I saw her walking across the square, legs buckled and body thin and torn. I never imagined he would use her to hurt someone else."

Oliver's stomach clenched as he recalled driving the police car into the Witch, right in front of Asher.

Asher looked at Oliver. "You did the right thing. Imagine how much more damage she would have done under his command—how many more people might have died." He pulled another history book from the pile. "This was always one of my favorites. US history reads like a dark fairy tale—brother fighting brother, metal birds dropping fire from the sky, thousands marching as far as the eye can see."

Asher set the book aside and sifted through the pile once more. "It's still here!" He grinned as he pulled a miniature leather-bound book of fairy tales from beneath the stack of heavy textbooks.

He stuffed the book into his back pocket and stood. "We can go now."

Aymes and Clockmaker were waiting for them

outside, and they all descended the staircase and criss-crossed down to the main floor of the town hall.

A noise came from the other side of the double doors leading to the meeting hall.

"There are more of you?" Oliver asked.

Aymes crossed the room and opened the door. Most of the room had been cleared of the wooden benches, and upon closer inspection, Oliver realized several of them had been used to bar the doors leading outside. Straw lined half the floor, and a stack of blankets and pillows sat in one corner. The room housed ten or fifteen people, most of whom were lined up at a table under the throne where Simon had once perched. A man scooped gray mush from a stockpot and splattered it into serving bowls.

"We go out and scavenge what we can during the day, but we can barely keep enough to feed them," Aymes said.

"What about the blood seekers? How many are there?"

"Twenty, maybe thirty, but they've started to dwindle with the cold and lack of food. We thought they would turn on each other, and some have, but others have formed packs. We think they are hunting the remaining townspeople who have scattered to the forest."

Oliver and Asher received stares from two children

playing with a makeshift ball. Asher waved, but this friendly gesture frightened them, and they retreated to the corner of the room.

"The blood seekers killed their parents," Aymes said, "but not before they squirreled the little ones away under the floorboards. They're the only two children left in Briarwood, at least as far as we know. Several may still live on the outskirts, but it's too dangerous to go after them. Isn't worth the risk."

"Isn't worth the risk?" Oliver asked. "Seems a little cold."

"You saw the blood seekers. They are not covered with their own blood. Even if we could find more townsfolk, odds are none of us would make it back to the hall."

"So you're just waiting here? For what?"

"To see who starves first, us or them," Aymes replied.

CHAPTER EIGHT

P an rooted his nose through the straw-covered floor and emerged victorious, with a hand-stitched doll between his teeth. He carried the toy back to the little girl, who had thrown it, but she struggled to pry it from Pan's mouth.

A woman noticed Pan with the doll and marched over from the far end of the room. "It took a week for your mother to make that doll, and I'll take a cold dip in the pond before I let that mongrel destroy it."

As she pulled the doll out of the girl's hands, Pan leapt at the woman's legs, pleading for her to return the toy. When the girl cried, though, he turned and ran to her, sticking his cold nose in her face and licking her tears. She giggled again and wrapped her arms around the tiny pup.

Oliver sat next to Izzy and Asher on the straw floor

in the Briarwood hall. The adults had cleaned up lunch and were lounging around, some making small talk and others playing games with odd-looking decks of cards. Life in the hall must have been boring, sitting and waiting for the next blood-seeker attack. He wondered if the townspeople found any joy in the leisure, considering how difficult their lives must have been under Simon's rule.

Simon's throne overhead was an austere platform bordered with intricate metal wheels on either side, and it sat in odd contrast to the straw floor. The room's interior reminded Oliver of the old bombed-out cathedrals in Europe. Although Simon had been gone for only a year, the town looked as though it had crumbled centuries before.

"I knew Briarwood was real," Izzy said. "I could see it from my house, for Pete's sake, but to see it up close is extraordinary."

"If only it wasn't surrounded by bloodthirsty murderers," Oliver said.

"Well, you can't have it all, I guess," Izzy replied with a sly smile.

The little boy Oliver had seen earlier was staring at Nekko, who'd huddled close to Izzy. He pulled a loose piece of straw from the floor and tried to entice the cat to chase it, but Nekko remained a disinterested lump.

"Move it back and forth." Izzy made an *s* pattern with an index finger.

The boy wiggled the piece of straw as Izzy instructed.

Nekko fought the urge to pounce at first, seeming overwhelmed by the large group of people in the room. Finally, the boy wiggled the straw just right, and Nekko slapped her paw down, trapping the straw underneath. The boy pulled it away and giggled then started the process over again.

Gideon tapped Oliver on a shoulder and motioned for him to follow.

"I'll be back," Oliver said as he stood to follow Gideon.

Gideon led him to a workroom, where Aymes sat at a long table, leaning over an old parchment map of the town, with Anna and the Clockmaker on the other side.

"He was just talking about doing another supply run," Anna said as Aymes gestured for Oliver to take a seat.

Aymes leaned across the table. "We have opened every cupboard and searched every storeroom in this place. We are running low on grain, and if we don't gather more soon, we won't have enough to feed those in the hall. Help us gather more supplies, and we'll help you reclaim your town."

"Where are the supplies?" Oliver asked.

Aymes pointed at the parchment map. The buildings had been drawn in ink, with the town square at the center. The briars were lined with inked skulls, and the map faded into nothingness on the other side. Behind the square lay several rows of houses.

"Stole this from Simon's quarters. Quite something, isn't it? We've been working our way through the dry goods stored in the houses just behind the hall, rummaging for barrels of rice and flour hidden in the root cellars." He traced a finger along the row of houses. "These have been picked clean. As we travel farther and farther away from the hall, the risk of confrontation with a blood seeker or two becomes greater. We lost two men in last week's scavenging. Every loss makes it more difficult to carry on and means one less for protecting our town hall and the people in it."

He pointed at a building behind the row of houses. "We keep a supply of grain in the storehouse across town. We haven't touched it, so hopefully it's still intact. We'll have to sneak between the houses to get to it, and we haven't been that far in some time, so there's no telling how many blood seekers may be waiting for us. But if we can access it, we will have enough supplies for the foreseeable future."

Oliver traced the map with his eyes. Buildings

surrounded the storehouse, leaving nearly unlimited cracks and crevices in which the evil creatures could hide.

"This is suicide," Oliver said.

"Either that, or we wait here to starve. I'd much rather face death head-on than watch our people wither away to nothing," Aymes replied.

Oliver leaned over the map once more. "And if I help you, how are you going to help me?"

"We'll march up the hill and lop the Collector's head off," Aymes replied. "Well, I'll leave that task to Gideon."

Gideon nodded.

"No offense, but how can you help us when you can hardly step outside without a blood seeker jumping down your throat?"

Aymes sneered. "I've made a more than reasonable offer. I see the way you carry that weapon, and your stance is hardly that of a hardened warrior. The blood seekers are dwindling. I know not how many are left, but we've been picking away at them slowly but surely. We're both in troubled positions—I would be a fool not to admit it—but we can help each other achieve our goals."

"Forget the storehouse," Oliver said. "If you help me, you'll have no reason to stay here. You can take the entire town to Christchurch. The barrier's broken, and there's nothing keeping you here."

Aymes furrowed his brow. "Briarwood may be in a sorry state now, but this is our home. We've fought too long to give up now. No, you help us keep our town alive, and we'll help you reclaim yours."

Oliver realized the futility of Aymes's plan. Even if he could save Briarwood, the barrier had been broken, and modern society, or the police for that matter, would surely come knocking.

He looked at Gideon, who sat back in his chair and folded his arms. He cocked his head to one side and raised his eyebrows.

"How can I help?" Anna asked. "I can't just let you go off, getting yourself killed."

"This is men's work, and Oliver here hardly qualifies as is. Go upstairs, and perhaps one of the women can show you how to sew," Aymes replied with a chuckle.

Anna's face shifted from pale to crimson.

Aymes turned toward Oliver to speak, but before he could utter another word, Anna reached for a metal bolt on the shelf next to her and flung it at him, striking him in the side of the head.

"Ah!" Aymes shouted as he pressed a palm against his temple and winced. "What was that for?"

Anna slammed her fists on the table. "What do you

think it was for? I'll have you know I could have taken that blood seeker in the square myself while Oliver was fumbling for his gun."

"Relax, woman. I meant nothing by it," Aymes replied. He looked up at Anna. "If you want to help, we'll need someone in the tower to keep an eye out for the seekers."

Anna folder her arms. "Not exactly what I had in mind, but I'll take it."

The Clockmaker crossed the room and grabbed a metal object from a shelf nearby. "Here, you'll need this, then."

"What is it?" Anna asked.

The piece was made of curved metal that reminded Oliver of a miniature French Horn.

"Blow through it," the Clockmaker replied.

Anna put her lips to the tip of the contraption and blew, filling the room with a piercing whistle. Oliver clasped his hands to his ears until Anna stopped.

"If you see anything approaching, give this a toot, and they'll hear you all the way down at the storehouse."

"How many blood seekers are in the area?" Oliver asked.

"We've cleared most of the square, but for all we know, twenty or thirty could still be hiding in the neighborhood and the outskirts of town," Aymes replied.

"Twenty or thirty?" Oliver asked, more to himself than anyone else. He envisioned the three of them surrounded by blood seekers and wondered whether he would rather face whatever horror awaited them back home than be ripped apart by an army of blood-thirsty Briarwood villagers.

Once Gideon had sharpened his weapon and Anna had reached the lantern room upstairs, Oliver, Gideon, and Aymes left the safety of the basement to retrieve the supplies.

Oliver had never seen the other side of town before. His experiences had been limited to the square, where he'd spent much of his time either tied up or locked away in some form or another.

He looked back at the lantern room and saw Anna peering over its edge, perched behind the corroded copper frame. They crossed the backstreets, passing demolished houses and toppled streetlamps.

Unlike the other buildings in Briarwood, the storehouse had been constructed of long wooden timbers and somewhat reminded Oliver of an old log cabin. The thatched roof sat heavy on the structure and appeared to be nearly a foot thick. The building had been constructed in front of a field now covered in a thick layer of undisturbed snow.

The door to the storehouse had been left open, and they approached cautiously, although the snow crunched loudly under their feet despite their best efforts to step lightly.

Gideon approached the entrance, sword drawn and ready to strike.

Aymes pulled Oliver back several feet from the door. "If that contraption fires bullets, I suggest preparing to fire," he whispered.

Oliver quietly cocked a hammer of his gun blade and raised it in the door's direction while Aymes pulled an arrow from his quiver.

"No more guns in Simon's chambers?" Oliver asked.

"No more ammunition," Aymes replied. "Ran out months ago. I've been learning the bow, but I still miss now and then."

"That's reassuring," Oliver replied.

Gideon pushed the door open and backed away.

They waited a moment, but no creatures emerged from the storehouse.

Gideon beckoned the others to join him and stepped inside the building, still brandishing his broadsword and listening intently for any signs of a blood seeker.

Oliver's eyes took a moment to adjust as he entered the building, and the bright snow gave way to a brown earthen floor lit by nothing more than the afternoon sun creeping through the entrance and bouncing off dust particles floating in the air. Wooden barrels filled the room from wall to wall, probably one hundred or more.

"How many do we need?" Oliver asked.

Aymes laughed. "We need all of them. We can move one, maybe two." He nodded toward a barrel. "Try to move it."

Oliver stepped forward and slid his weapon into its sheath. He gripped the barrel at the top and tried to shift it. "How much do these weigh?"

Aymes pointed at Gideon. "At least one of him."

Oliver figured Gideon might have weighed three hundred pounds.

"There should be a cart out back," Aymes said. "If we carry two, that should last us for a week, maybe two if we're careful."

Gideon removed the bar from the barn door on the opposite end of the building. As he pushed it open, careful not to make unnecessary noise, a shrill whistle echoed in the distance.

"Blood seekers," Aymes said.

Oliver looked around but saw no motion in his periphery. "Where?"

"Must be on the other side of town, maybe in the square. Come on—we must hurry. You and Gideon load the cart, and I will check the front of the building for seekers."

"Shouldn't we leave it?" Oliver asked.

"Leave it, and we starve. We're taking it back. Best be on the lookout, boy."

Oliver followed Gideon to the back of the building while Aymes went through the front door onto the street.

As Gideon approached the other side of the cart to grab its long wooden handle, a flash of metal caught Oliver's eye as it struck Gideon's calf. Gideon fell to his knees and opened his mouth as though to cry out, but no sound emerged.

A blood seeker crawled from behind the cart and raised his blade to strike again. Gideon caught his arm, and the knife stopped just short of his chest.

When Oliver raised his weapon, the blood seeker pushed off from the cart and pinned Gideon to the ground, still trying to press the knife into him.

As the two wrestled, Oliver hesitated, unsure if his aim was good enough to hit the correct target. Before he could decide, Gideon grabbed the blood seeker by the neck, his hand completely wrapping around the seeker's throat. He slammed the seeker's other hand against the side of the cart until the knife fell to the ground. Oliver kicked the knife away as Gideon tightened his grip on the seeker's neck.

The seeker panicked and fell backward behind the cart. Eventually, he stopped flailing and lay limp in the snow.

"Are you all right?" Oliver asked.

Blood dripped from Gideon's calf, and he ripped a piece of fabric from his sleeve and tied it tightly around his leg.

Aymes poked his head out of the doorway. "Are you coming?" He looked at the dead blood seeker then at Gideon, who rose to his feet. "Quickly, before more come."

The cart's large wooden wheels shifted clumsily on their axles as Gideon pulled it inside. He removed the wooden lid of a barrel and ran his hand through the grain before putting the cap back on. He smacked the top of the barrel with his hand and gestured for Aymes to help him lift it onto the cart.

Oliver tried to help but was certain he was only getting in the way. Once they'd loaded two barrels onto the cart, they ventured through the back door as Gideon pulled it behind them.

Oliver marveled at the size of the town. His eyes traced the winding dirt streets as they returned to the hall. He'd assumed Briarwood was a quaint little village, grand town hall aside, but the place seemed to stretch quite a ways into the forest.

They reached the corner of the square, and the

shrill screech of Anna's whistle continued. Oliver looked up into the lantern room and saw Anna standing, whistle to her lips but staring off into the distance. When she turned and saw them reach the square, she disappeared from the window.

"What's that girl on about?" Aymes asked, clearly annoyed.

They rushed as fast as they could with the heavy wooden cart until they reached the side door. By the time the Clockmaker let them inside, Anna had already reached the workroom.

"Want to tell us what that was all about?" Oliver asked.

"Izzy's house is burning," she said, out of breath.

Oliver's heart dropped.

They raced through the workroom, and Anna grabbed Izzy and Asher from the meeting hall, then the six of them rushed upstairs to the lantern room.

"What's going on?" Izzy asked.

Oliver caught a flicker from the top of the hill across the field.

The others rushed to the broken window, bracing themselves against the cold.

Flames shot up from the yellow-sided Victorian at the top of the hill. Fire ripped through the turret—Izzy's studio—and smoke drifted over the field in spiraling black plumes.

"I can't believe it." Oliver choked back tears.

Izzy said nothing but stood with a hand cupped over her mouth, tears streaming down her cheeks.

"We have to go back. They'll burn the entire town. The Collector is sending a message," Oliver said.

Aymes looked out at the burning house. "Smells like a trap to me. He is trying to draw you back."

"What are we going to do?" Oliver asked.

"We?" Aymes asked.

Oliver turned around just in time to see Gideon jab Aymes on the back of the shoulder.

"We helped you, and now it's time for you to fulfill your end of the bargain," Oliver said, fists clenched.

Aymes smirked. "We will set our own trap, then."

CHAPTER NINE

The group returned to the workroom and gathered around one of the wooden tables. Izzy sat at the end of a bench, bent over with head in hands while Anna comforted her.

"Izzy, I'm so sorry," she said.

"Just stuff," Izzy replied.

"What?"

Izzy sat up and wiped her eyes. "No one was hurt, and we can replace everything in that house. I'm just glad we got out while we could."

"How many are we up against?" Aymes asked.

"Just one, I think, and whatever he's got hidden on that train," Oliver replied.

"Train?" Aymes asked.

"The train parked at Christchurch station."

"What is a train?" Aymes asked.

Oliver's mouth hung open as he contemplated how to explain. "A large metal cart that travels around on tracks."

Aymes met him with a blank stare. "One man and his cart? That's it?"

Oliver looked down at the table, somewhat embarrassed.

"If he's waiting for you at the top of the hill, take your weapon and shoot him," Aymes added casually.

"It's not that simple. He wouldn't let me bring my weapon on the train, and he's starting the fire with his hands somehow. He's got to be an Unnatural."

"An Unnatural?" Aymes asked.

"He's using magic, like Simon and the Witch."

Aymes's face went pale.

"We can draw him into Briarwood and let the blood seekers take care of him," the Clockmaker said as if the solution was obvious. "We'll solve two problems at once. If the blood seekers can't do it, at least we'll be rid of some."

"How are we going to do that?" Oliver asked.

The Clockmaker stood from the table and crossed to one of his workbenches. He brought over a shiny metal ball and handed it to Oliver with a winding key. The ball was the same as the one Aymes and Gideon had used to distract the blood seekers when Oliver crossed into Briarwood.

The device was composed of several curved metal plates that covered an intricate clockwork core.

"Wind it," the Clockmaker said.

Oliver inserted the key into a hole in the middle of one of the plates and twisted. The gears shifted inside, and the plates tightened around them.

"Now press a panel and cover your ears."

Oliver did so and set the orb onto the table next to them. With a subtle ticking, the device sat for a few seconds before a shrill ring filled the air.

"Draws them like a charm," the Clockmaker said, shouting over the ringing.

"Like an alarm clock," Oliver said. "What are they called?"

"Clangers," the Clockmaker replied. "Take one in your pocket and drop it once you reach the square on your way back."

Oliver picked up one of the metal orbs and stuffed it into a coat pocket, leaving an obvious lump.

"You don't think this is a little suspicious?"

Aymes laughed. "Show him the new contraption— the beetle-looking creature."

The Clockmaker tapped his fingers together in excitement. "Yes, this occasion would be perfect to test it!" He walked to a workbench at the back of the room and motioned Oliver and Asher to join him.

"I have so much time to tinker now the shop is no

more. We know the blood seekers will run to the clangers, but they quickly lose interest once they find them."

He pulled some cloth off a larch lump in the middle of the table.

"I've tried a few different versions, but this one seems the most promising," he said. "I've made a small fleet."

After a few seconds, Oliver realized the mishmash of gears, cogs, and metal made up a clockwork spider of sorts. Like the clanger, it had a winding mechanism in the center, but this device had long spindly metal legs.

The Clockmaker picked up the contraption and pulled another metal key from his pocket. After a few cranks, he set the device on the floor and flipped a brass switch on its back.

The legs of the mechanical arachnid began to move, and the Clockmaker set the device on the floor. The creature skittered across the stone, much faster than Oliver had expected. The spider climbed over the uneven stones until it reached the wall.

"What's its purpose?" Oliver asked.

The Clockmaker crossed the room, picked up the device, then returned to the table. He flicked the brass switch, and when the spider's legs stopped, he placed it on the table. He pulled a clanger from the workbench then snapped it onto the creature's back.

"It's capable of traveling much farther than one can throw. Keeps the seeker on the move. We let one of these loose and have it run away from the square and into the woods behind the hall. This will give you enough time to cross the briars."

"How long do they last?" Oliver asked.

"A few minutes."

"But how do we draw the Collector to Briarwood?"

Both Gideon and Aymes looked at Asher.

"Taunt him with what he most desires," Aymes replied.

"I can do it," Asher said. "Considering all of this is because of me, the least I can do is help."

"No. Absolutely no way," Oliver replied.

Asher scowled. "I should have a say in this too. If others are risking their lives to protect me, I ought to help."

Oliver looked down at the table and remembered his conversation with Anna before his drive to the train station. "You're right. I'm sorry. But if you go to him, he has no reason to come to Briarwood. He'll take you and leave. If we get him back here, we can stop him. I can convince him to come—I know it."

Asher's expression softened. "All right. But if this doesn't work, I am going to the train, and I'm not asking first."

"We don't have time for debate. Do you want to wait until your entire town is scorched?" Aymes asked.

"Just promise me you'll have my back," Oliver said.

"If the spiders don't bring the blood seekers, I'll be ready with an arrow," Aymes replied. "I may be able to hit him from the tower."

* * *

UPSTAIRS, Aymes scanned the town square for blood seekers, and once the coast was clear, he dropped a piece of fabric to signal those in the workroom. Oliver stepped through the side door of the building and out into the snow.

Gideon followed Oliver closely, positioning himself in a vacant storefront on the other side of the square.

The place was eerily silent, aside from the crunch of snow underneath his boots. Oliver pulled his coat tighter but had left his weapons behind. He wanted the Collector to think he was making a serious offer, and weapons might complicate the situation.

As he reached the edge of the woods, he stood for a moment and watched the house blazing at the top of the hill. His life in Christchurch flashed before his eyes, and the only thing keeping him together was the knowledge that everyone who lived in that house was safely tucked away in the Briarwood town hall. As he crossed the field and climbed the hill to Izzy's, black smoke swirled overhead as flames hissed and crackled, roaring from Izzy's studio window as they turned her life's work to ash. His initial sadness was replaced by rage at the senseless destruction and death the Collector had brought upon the town.

The Collector had dusted off an old lawn chair from the back porch and posted himself just a few feet from the house, looking down the hill as Oliver approached. He'd propped his feet on an old tree stump. His right sleeve was rolled up to his elbow, and his arm was bright red and burned. His nonchalance—sitting peacefully while the house burned and crumbled behind him—made Oliver furious.

Cold wind whipped against Oliver's back while the heat from the fire beat against his chest. Oliver tried to step toward the Collector, but the man was perched impossibly close to the blaze. Embers hissed as they hit the snow, leaving specks in the white like poisonous raindrops.

"I assumed a little bonfire might pull you out of hiding," the man said. "I thought we had a deal—deliver Asher by dawn, and I'd be on my way. Dawn has come and gone, my friend." He gestured for Oliver to take off his coat once more.

"You didn't have to do this." Oliver unzipped his

coat and dropped it in the snow, showing he was hiding no weapons.

"*Have to,* no—I thoroughly enjoyed it, though. You're lucky I decided to spare the rest of the town, for now. Where is the boy?"

Oliver stood silent, overcome with a mix of rage and grief.

"Not very smart, are you?" the Collector asked. "If you don't tell me, I will destroy this pathetic excuse for a town and burn down every house until I find him."

"And you'll still come up empty-handed." Oliver swallowed hard. "But I'll take you to him if you spare the town."

The Collector perked up. "I hoped this might change your tune, but color me surprised. So where is he?"

Oliver pointed to the woods. "Just on the other side. In Simon's town."

The Collector grinned. "I'd always hoped I'd get to see it. Thought the man was crazy at first, promising eternal life for a second chance at his. If one of my associates hadn't met him in the clink—"

Oliver clenched a fist. "Spare me the story. Do you want Asher or not?" He picked up his coat and slipped his arms through the sleeves.

"All right—no need for an attitude," the Collector replied. "Lead the way."

As Oliver led the Collector through the snow, the man's idle chatter scraped Oliver's ears like nails on a chalkboard. He wanted to turn and strangle him for taking away Izzy's home and everything she'd worked so hard for. Oliver found solace in the thought that the blood seekers awaited them on the other side of the briars.

They stepped through the broken brambles, and when they reached the square, the Collector's eyes traced the dilapidated buildings and charred town hall. "This is the 'kingdom' Simon referred to? It's a pile of rubble."

A flash of shiny metal caught Oliver's eye at the edge of the square as a clockwork spider skittered around the corner of the hall. Another came from the door of the Clockmaker's shop.

"What the hell are those?" The Collector looked down at one of the strange objects, unsure of what to make of it.

The spider let out a shrill ring as it passed midway through the square.

The Collector backed away as the second device triggered, and he turned toward the woods as the creature passed.

Oliver ran, sprinting through the deep snow to the door on the other side of the hall. After he pounded on the door a few times, the Clockmaker pulled it open and let him inside.

Izzy and Anna were waiting nearby and rushed over as he entered.

"Are you all right?" Izzy asked.

"It worked," Oliver replied.

They had an obscured view of the square through the thin workroom windows.

The Collector gripped one of the writhing creatures. "What kind of game is this? You think these toys will help you?"

He slammed the spider onto the ground, and pieces of the device broke loose although the clanger continued to ring.

"Where did you go?" the Collector shouted. "You're just prolonging the inevitable! Bring me the boy with the magic blood!"

He twisted around in search of Oliver.

"What are you playing at?" he shouted. "If I have to track you down, I will make you regret it!"

As the Collector walked toward the hall, Oliver heard a shout from the far end of town, in the distance behind the dilapidated Clockmaker's shop where Gideon was hiding. The Collector must have heard it, too, because he jerked around and stepped toward that side of the square.

"Don't play with me."

The noise had drawn the attention of several blood seekers, who emerged from behind a row of houses. Eventually, they squeezed between the clothing shop and the Clockmaker's shop, next to it.

"Bad night out on the town? Go on a bit of a bender, did ya?" he asked the first blood seeker who rounded the corner, caked in dried blood and barefoot in the snow, with four others following.

"Is this a joke?"

The blood seekers hobbled toward him, fanning out as they approached.

"I assure you, I'm not the man you want to mess with!"

This is it, Oliver thought. *They'll rip him to pieces.*

One blood seeker stumbled forward.

"Guess my suit's ruined anyway," the Collector said, pulling something from his pants pocket—the same lighter he'd fiddled with earlier.

As the seeker lunged, the Collector flicked the flint wheel in his left hand and held the flame to the palm of his right. Fire burst from his palm, catching the unsuspecting blood seeker square in the face. He stopped short and screamed, trying to put the fire out with his hands.

The others moved in, and the Collector waved his hand across their paths, catching each of them in a fan of flames.

When the burst died, five blood seekers lay on the ground, snow hissing around them as their bodies burned. The Collector screamed in agony as he tried to pat out the fire running up his right arm.

"Anybody else?" His shouting had become raspy and wild.

The Collector's arm was bright red, and his suit had burned to the shoulder. The more fire he created, it appeared, the more he himself suffered. His head turned in the direction of the shiny metal bauble that had brought the mob over to the Clockmaker's shop.

He knows where Gideon is hiding.

As the Collector lifted his hand to send another explosive fireball, an arrow struck the Collector through the shin, and he screamed in agony. Before Aymes could fire a second shot from the tower, the Collector sent a burst toward him and limped behind the base of the destroyed statue in the square.

"I don't have time for this!" He stumbled as he pulled the arrow from his calf. He removed a vial from his pocket and grunted as he pressed the dropper into his open wound.

Asher's blood. Although Simon had destroyed one of the large fish tanks of Asher's blood in an attempt to bring himself back from the dead, the other had gone missing, along with the specimen jars from The Parlor's display.

Once he'd drained the vial, leaving no more for his burn wounds, the Collector raised his arm as though preparing to send another burst of fire toward Aymes in the tower, but screams from another nearby blood seeker distracted him.

"Midnight!" he yelled. "I may not be able to get to you or the boy in that fortress of yours, but Christchurch has nowhere to hide. You have until midnight to come to the train station, or I burn the entire town and everyone in it to the ground."

The Collector sent another burst of flame toward the tower, giving him just enough cover to limp toward the tree line. Somehow, Aymes fired off another shot, but the arrow fell short and disappeared in the snow.

Two blood seekers approached from the corner of the square, but by the time they reached the tree line, the Collector had already crossed into the field.

As the seekers searched for the source of the commotion, Gideon appeared from the doorway of the Clockmaker's shop. He raised his broadsword and sneaked up on them, striking the first seeker in the back, then the other in the chest as he turned around. Then Gideon crossed the square to the town hall.

"Are you all right?" Oliver asked as Gideon entered the workroom.

Gideon nodded and wiped his forehead.

Aymes barreled into the workroom a few minutes

later. "I can't believe I missed the shot. That damned tower is just too tall."

"You tried," Oliver replied. "The Collector said we had till midnight before he burns the town. He'll be able to destroy all of Christchurch within a few minutes with *that* kind of power."

"He might be able to destroy the old shops on the square, but fire means nothing to giant slabs of stone," the Clockmaker said.

"Huh?"

"You could bring your townspeople to Briarwood. Keep them in the town hall—right here. They'll be safe behind these walls."

"Are you mad?" Aymes asked. "Bring the entire town here? Who knows how many blood seekers are still out there? We'd be lucky if we got anyone through the woods without being slaughtered."

"He is just one man, and the blood seekers are mindless animals. We have four or five men here who can handle a weapon if needed—perhaps not soldiers, but still..."

"He is but one man who sends flames spewing from his hands, and they are but a mindless pack, wanting nothing more than to cut us open and drink our blood. Your plan is pure lunacy!" Aymes yelled.

"Then we sit here and watch the man slaughter

everyone in the town on the hill. Can you live with that blood on your hands?"

"Take me to him," Asher said.

"What?"

"I'll go to the Collector."

"Are you nuts? If we do that, what's all this for?" Oliver replied.

"You promised if the other plans didn't work, you'd let me try. How many chances do you think we'll have before he torches the town? He's not stupid. If you take me to the train, maybe someone can get a clear shot at him when he opens the door."

"I can't let you do that," Oliver replied.

"It isn't your choice," Asher shot back.

"I think Asher's right," Anna said. "We've tried running, and we've tried leading him to the blood seekers. We have to give Asher's plan a try."

Aymes laughed. "You have all lost your heads."

Oliver looked at Asher. "Are you sure?"

"It's worth a try."

Izzy stood from the bench and approached, pulling the bright flare gun from underneath her jacket. "Could this help?"

CHAPTER TEN

The sun sank behind the horizon as they put the plan into action. The Clockmaker kept an eye on the square from ground level, while Aymes perched in the tower above them. After several practice shots, he managed to pick off two blood seekers who wandered into the square, then Oliver, Anna, Asher, and Gideon stepped through the side door and out into Briarwood. This time, Oliver kept his weapon in easy reach, and his fingers twitched as he ran them along its handle. Anna carried her bat, and Asher had tucked the flare gun in his belt behind his back.

They passed the bodies of Aymes's victims then the temporary winter graves of the seekers the Collector had dispatched earlier.

Oliver looked back at the tower and Aymes's silhouette, barely visible in the light of dusk. Once they stepped into the woods, they left the range of Aymes's protection to brave the wilderness alone.

Gideon's limp had improved since the seekers' earlier attack, but the sound of his steps was still uneven as he crossed the briars, a light crunch followed by a heavier thump.

They stopped at the edge of the woods once they'd broken through to the other side and Izzy's house came into view.

Oliver longed for the bakery—longed for the warm fire in Izzy's cheery yellow house, the house that had been reduced to a pile of smoldering rubble. The sorrow for Izzy's loss left an ache deep in his bones.

As the group stepped into the field, Oliver heard a rustling in the woods behind him.

A blood seeker had followed them to the edge of the woods but stopped short of the dead briar patch.

"He won't cross," Oliver said under his breath.

"What makes you think that?" Anna asked.

"Just wishful thinking," Oliver replied.

The seeker growled and looked down at the patch in front of him. He took a step forward, aligning his ragged boot with a large shoe print Gideon had left in the snow. The briars crunched as the seeker traced Gideon's steps, reaching halfway across the patch.

"Shoot him," Anna said.

Oliver raised his gun sword and clicked one of the

hammers. He trained the tip of the sword at the blood seeker's chest and pulled the trigger, but the bullet missed its mark. The blood seeker picked up speed as he crossed.

"It's been a while," Oliver said as he frantically cocked the other hammer. He breathed in and exhaled as he pulled the trigger, this time striking the blood seeker in a shoulder, sending him off course and screaming.

As the seeker recovered, Gideon stepped in to finish the job, bringing his sword down.

The blood seeker's scream echoed through the woods, followed by the calls of others in response.

Limbs snapped on the other side of the briars as a group of seekers approached.

"Do you think the others will catch on?" Asher asked.

"We shouldn't wait to find out. Let's get out of here," Anna replied.

Oliver reloaded his weapon as they jogged up the hill toward Izzy's.

The hives had been spared—that much he could see from the field. Amidst the chaos, Oliver found it oddly reassuring that the tiny communities had survived the smoke and flame.

Oliver and Anna took a quick detour around the house, and he tried to cement his memories of the place deep within his mind. The fire had left little intact, and even the porte cochère had collapsed atop Izzy's new station wagon, crushing it under a pile of burned timbers and scorched shingles. Gideon waited patiently until they were ready to move on.

Oliver checked his watch as they sneaked behind the police station.

Eric was sitting alone at a police radio under the dim glow of a desk lamp. When he saw them, he threw his headset on the table and pushed his chair back.

"I can't believe it," he said, looking up at the hulking man clutching a broadsword. "Please tell me he's on our side."

"This is Gideon," Oliver replied.

"Where is Izzy? Is she all right?"

"She's at the town hall in Briarwood," Oliver replied. "She's fine for now and in a lot better position than we are. How's Gary?"

"He's fine, thank God—well, as fine as a guy can be who's just been stabbed. He'll live. He's over at the hall with the rest of the town. I was just about to head back over there. After Izzy's house, we thought it best we keep everyone in the same place—a place that's not made of wood. Thought we'd have a better chance of protecting them."

"Then why are you here?" Oliver asked.

"Trying to get a message through to Amberley. It's useless, though—still static."

Eric rubbed his chin. "I can't believe this is happening. Mitch is dead, Gary's stabbed, Izzy's house is burned to the ground. It's my job to protect this town, but we see how well that's going." He put his head in his hands. "I'd shoot that little weasel myself if I could get close enough."

"We tried to lure him into Briarwood. We thought the blood seekers would take care of him. He nearly toasted Gideon here."

Gideon nodded.

Eric lifted his head. "Blood seekers?" When Oliver started to speak, Eric held up a hand. "No, never mind —one evil nemesis at a time. Please tell me you have a plan."

"We're going to take the train," Anna replied.

"Take the train? Have you lost your mind? You've seen what that man's capable of."

Asher stepped forward. "He came here for me, and I'm going to give him what he wants."

"What do you mean?"

"I'm the bait. When he opens the door to take me, the rest of us will be waiting."

"And if that doesn't work?" Eric asked.

"Then we take the townspeople to Briarwood," Oliver replied.

"To the town in the woods?"

"They've fortified their town hall. Ours may be made of stone, but Briarwood's hall is practically a castle. We'll be safer there."

"Why would they have fortified the town hall?" Eric asked.

"Those blood seekers you didn't want me to explain—but it's take our chances with them or stay here and burn alive."

Eric rubbed his temples. "What do we need to do?"

"Where is the Collector?" Oliver asked.

"Who?"

"That's his name. He told us to call him the Collector."

Eric smirked. "Of course he did. I assume he's back at the station, but we haven't seen him since the fire at Izzy's. He comes out for short bursts of time, but that train is locked up tight. We can't get in."

"We'll need to get to the hall first. From there, we'll need a few townspeople to help with the plan, if we can get anyone to agree to it."

Eric nodded, rose from his chair, and walked to the window looking out onto the snow-covered square. "I trust you. Just tell me what you need."

Hidden by the haze of the storm, they crept across the square, and an explosion of chatter spewed out into the winter air as Oliver pulled open one of the doors to the hall. The townsfolk had rearranged the chairs and sat in small circles, talking nervously.

The mayor rushed toward them and wrapped his arms around Anna.

"Are you all right? Where is Izzy? What happened in the woods?"

Anna said nothing but squeezed him tightly with her muscular-baker arms.

"Izzy is all right," Oliver replied. "We've been holed up in the town in the woods. They are safe for now."

"Why was the loudspeaker calling for you?" Madeline broke through the chatter and strode to the front of the room.

"The man's looking for Asher," Oliver replied.

"The odd boy who's been staying with you?" she asked. "He's the reason for all of this?"

Uneasiness spread in the pit of Oliver's stomach, and he tried to swallow the lump in his throat.

"That's true, but—" Oliver started.

"Where is he?" Madeline interrupted.

The crowd parted around Asher, who had backed up against the wall.

"Let's not lose our heads," Oliver replied.

"Lose our heads?" Madeline was taken aback. "No, no... We have to keep him safe. We can't let that miscreant waltz off with him to who knows where. He may not be the most social citizen of Christchurch, but he's a citizen all the same."

Oliver's mouth hung agape as he gradually comprehended her words. "So you're saying you want to help him?"

Madeline's cheeks flashed red. "Of course we want to help him. He's a member of this town. We can't just let a bully wander in here and take over. We won't let him get away with killing Mitch or burning Isabelle's house. We've worked too hard to build this community, and we're not letting anyone take it away from us. Isn't that right?" She turned toward the crowd, who replied with a collective yawp.

"We have a plan," Oliver replied.

"Then please, tell us," Madeline said.

Madeline stuck two fingers in her mouth and whistled to quiet the crowd, an unladylike act that seemed uncharacteristic. All her snobbishness was gone, apparently.

"Thanks," Oliver said.

Grade-school Oliver came rushing back, and he found it difficult to stand up and speak in front of the room full of people even though he'd been able to brave the blood seekers and the Collector.

"I, um..." he started as the crowd gathered around. He was unsure of where to begin as the situation seemed so unreal.

"We're in trouble!" Anna shouted from the back of the room.

A nervous laugh trickled through the crowd.

Oliver settled on telling the God's honest truth. "The man who's been setting fire to the town—the Collector, he calls himself—is here for Asher. Some of you know the truth—that Asher has a special ability, but this ability is what's bringing these people to our doorstep. They want his blood. I'm not sure I understand it all myself, but his blood has special properties. There are people in this world with similar abilities, but none as special as Asher's. The man with the orange hair—he's another. It's why he's so dangerous. I know this sounds insane, but he can shoot flames from his hands."

"I've seen it," Eric chimed in. "And many of you have seen it too. We've got to get out of denial. What Oliver's saying is true."

Oliver cleared his throat. "If we don't deliver Asher to the train by midnight, he will burn the town, and he's more than capable. He's killed before, and I'm sure he'll do it again."

"That's reassuring," Madeline said sarcastically. "What do we do?"

"We give him exactly what he wants." Oliver continued, "Our other plans haven't worked, so we're going to use Asher as a lure to coax him out of the train and hope we have enough collective strength to outsmart and overpower him. He won't believe that I'd turn Asher in after I've fought so hard to keep him safe. But if some wily townspeople get fed up with the destruction and took matters into their own hands, that might be something the Collector buys. We need a few of you to pretend to capture us and bring us to the train. Once we're there, if we can lure him out, we'll need someone with good aim." Oliver nodded at Eric. "If that doesn't work, Gideon will be waiting to strike from the top of the train. If we have several plans in place, one of them is bound to pay off."

"Why don't we just leave town? Go to Amberley?" one of the townspeople asked.

"We tried to take Mitch, but the Collector has trapped us here, somehow. We're isolated from the outside world. The phones are down, but there's also a barrier surrounding us, kind of like the one that crumbled over Briarwood a few weeks ago."

Harry shot up from the crowd. "I, for one, think we should do as Oliver says. What do we have to lose?"

"Our town, if we don't try," another replied. "The boy's right! I'm not going to sit by and watch while that man burns our town to the ground. Let's show this bastard what we're made of."

"Well, what are we waiting for?" Madeline asked. "Let's go!"

"We have a backup plan," Oliver said. "If this doesn't work, there is a safe space in the town in the woods. As much as most of you would like to believe it doesn't exist, I know you've all seen it, peeking out above the trees. The hall with the tower is reinforced. Take the side entrance, and you'll find shelter there. But that plan has risks you should know about. There are people in the woods, scattered about Briarwood, who also seek to do us harm."

"Harm?" Madeline asked.

Oliver looked down at his shoes. "They want our blood. We'd have a better chance if we ran into one of them than the Collector, but we have to stay together."

"Now, wait a minute." A man named Tom stood up, despite the best efforts of his wife to hold him down. "First, you want us to believe a man can shoot fire from his hands. Now, you expect us to buy that there is a group of people waiting to suck our blood in the woods? And you expect us to eagerly march over there and be eaten alive? It all sounds like nonsense to me," he said.

"It's not nonsense, Tom." Eric stood to address the crowd. "We've seen things in the last year that can't be explained with reason. You've felt it, just as I did, when the Siren took over. We may have swept it under the rug with the Witch, but we can't continue to ignore it—

something evil is afoot in Christchurch. We have to trust him."

Tom thought for a moment then sat down next to his wife and folded his arms.

"If our plan to take the train succeeds, you'll be safe here. But if it falls apart, you have to be prepared to flee to Briarwood," Oliver said.

* * *

MADELINE LED a small pack of townspeople to the train station. Eric held Oliver's hands behind him, while Martin gripped Asher's. Anna hid at the edge of the station, just behind a closed news kiosk.

Gideon sneaked around back and lifted himself onto the top of the train, where he quietly crept from car to car until he rested above the door to the engine where Oliver had first met the Collector. The roof must have been slippery in the snow, but Gideon held firm and crouched, steadying himself above the door and preparing to strike.

Oliver and the others waited awkwardly for a moment or two, hoping the Collector would see them, but the metal sliding door remained shut.

"Hello?" Madeline yelled after the period of awkward silence. "We brought the boy," she shouted against the wind.

No response.

Madeline stepped up the metal stairs to the door and tapped on it with her wedding ring before stepping back into the snow.

"This is ridiculous," she said, crossing her arms and bracing herself against the cold.

A light flipped on in the front car, but the door stayed shut.

Martin pushed Asher toward the train car. "We've brought what you've asked for!" he shouted.

"Town turn over on ya, did it Oliver?" The Collector's voice boomed through the loudspeakers.

"We just want our town back and for you to leave," Martin said.

"They're a small price to pay," Madeline added, putting her acting skills to the test.

"Send Asher up here. Do whatever you want with the other boy—he's useless to me."

Gideon sat just above the closed door, waiting for his chance to strike, but the Collector refused to open it.

"What are you waiting for? Come here, boy."

Asher stepped forward but stopped short of the steps.

"Get up here and stand in front of the door!" The Collector was clearly growing impatient.

"No way I'm going to get a shot," Eric whispered to Oliver.

Asher looked back nervously and climbed the metal steps until his body blocked the door.

The door shot open, and the Collector yanked Asher inside, but not before Asher grabbed the flare gun from behind his back and fired.

A red burst of light framed Asher in silhouette, and he fell backward onto the platform. The Collector emerged from the car as hissing sparks and smoke from the flare lapped at his heels.

He stumbled forward and let out a yelp as Gideon pounced from behind, kicking him off the steps and onto the ground. Although the snow might have cushioned his fall somewhat, the man smacked his face hard on the concrete and lay motionless.

Gideon dropped from the train, crashing down upon the man. The Collector's lighter skittered across the ground, and Oliver rushed over and tucked it safely into a pocket.

The man tried to scramble free at first, letting out a slurred "Let me go" before passing out completely.

Gideon smirked as he pinned the man's hands down.

The Collector opened his eyes, but only the whites were visible. Tears formed in the corners as his irises appeared from behind his eyelids and seemed to pulse, shifting in hue from hazel to dark brown. As the man's aggressive expression faded, so did the shade of his skin.

Gideon let go of him and knelt back in disgust.

The Collector's body convulsed on the ground, his bright-red hair receding into his scalp and long brown locks shooting out in its place. His body seemed to absorb his clothing, and his hips expanded outward as his legs lengthened.

Gideon stood and looked at Oliver, who eyed the shifting form.

The short angry redhead had transformed into a woman, lying unconscious on the station floor. Oliver immediately recognized her tattered dress.

Gideon looked at Oliver as if waiting for instructions.

"Prop her up," he said, still unable to make sense of the scene.

Gideon slung the woman over a shoulder then set her against the lamppost, holding her arms securely behind her.

She let out a soft sigh as her head nodded against her chest.

The woman shook herself awake and shifted uncomfortably against the pole as Oliver and Eric knelt across from her. Her eyes darted between them as she struggled to make sense of her surroundings.

"Where am I?" she asked.

Oliver opened his mouth to speak, but she interrupted him.

"No, no! Don't tell me. Don't tell me anything. He might be listening."

"Who are you?" Oliver asked.

She ignored his question. "Is the boy safe?"

"At the moment," Oliver replied, looking back at Asher.

"We have little time." Tears streamed down her cheeks, and she struggled against Gideon's hold. "There's a key around my neck. It'll give you access to the train."

Oliver leaned in close and pulled the chain over her head. "How are you controlling the weather?"

"It's stolen magic," the woman said. "The flames, the storm—it's all stolen." Her eyes widened.

Magic left behind. He'd first learned about it from Ruby. Unnaturals could leave some of their powers behind in objects. The force field that once protected Briarwood was an example. Oliver still wasn't sure how it worked exactly, but the lighter must have been another magical artifact.

"He's got something on the train for the storm. I don't know where—he's hidden it from me, but if you find it, the storm will stop."

"Why are you helping us?" Oliver asked, still unsure of whether to trust the woman.

"I can't see everything," she said. "But I know he plans to kill you and destroy the town once you've given him the boy."

"But why?" Oliver asked. "Who is he?"

"I don't know," she replied. "He's been with me since I was a child, and the older I get, the more I sleep and the longer he's awake. You must have knocked him out."

"How did he find you?" Oliver asked.

"I found him, hiding under the foot of my bed."

"He was hiding under your bed?" Oliver asked.

"No, I was hiding. I'd made Father mad again. He tripped over one of my dolls on the floor. So I hid, and he reached out from the darkness and told me he could help. But he was inside me, in my head."

"I told my parents about him, but they didn't believe me. My father even tried to beat him out of me. He didn't like that. He told me to trust him, and I let him take control. He's always had a thing for fire. He went to the garage and pulled out the gasoline can that night—oh, how the house burned! I remember their screaming as I watched from the lawn. He'd shoved a doorstop under their bedroom door." Her eyes became red as she told the story.

Eric's face had gone pale.

"I tried to tell them I didn't do it. I could never have done something like that, but the police didn't believe me. They sent me away. I thought he was gone after the fire, but he came back. It was the guard—when the guard would..."

Oliver's stomach soured.

"He killed him—I'm sure of it—and when I woke up next, I was sleeping under an overpass. He escaped somehow, I don't know how, but he did."

Eric motioned for Gideon to loosen his grip.

"No!" the woman shouted. "If you let me go, you will all die."

"Where did he get the lighter?"

"Met a man in an institution a few years ago who liked to start fires too. They became good friends. He could start fires with gasoline, sure, but this man could start them with his hands. All he needed was a spark. That's his magic in the lighter. He stole it too."

"Why is he after Asher?"

The woman shrugged. "Power? Using the lighter has its costs, but the blood heals his wounds."

Oliver sat back on his heels. He swept his hand through a pile of snow and let the flakes fall through his fingers. He thought of the radio and the phones, all unusable since the storm started. The sudden blizzard and the isolation from neighboring towns seemed impossible.

"If the storm comes from stolen magic, who did he steal it from?" Oliver asked.

The woman looked down at her lap. "The woman who held the tanks of blood in her shop," she replied.

"Ruby?"

She nodded.

Oliver felt as if his veins had been injected with ice water. "Where is she?"

The woman remained silent.

Oliver reached over and shook her by the shoulders. "What did he do with her? Is she still alive?"

"I think we have a problem!" Anna shouted from the edge of the station.

Oliver turned toward her. "What?"

"I hear screaming coming from the town hall."

CHAPTER ELEVEN

A nna stood at the entrance of the station, overlooking the square as another shrill scream pierced the air.

Oliver pointed at the woman. "Get her inside," he told Gideon. He hopped up to the door of the first car and unlocked it with the Collector's key as Gideon helped the woman to her feet.

"Stay here with her," he added.

Anna took off toward the hall, and the rest of the pack followed close behind.

A pair of blood seekers were pulling at the building's rear door, and Oliver arrived just in time to see a metal flagpole pop out from the crack in the door and catch one on the side of the head. Eric pulled his pistol from his holster and fired five staccato shots, knocking each of the seekers to the ground.

As the seekers lay motionless, Eric tried to open the rear door, but the overzealous townsfolk inside mistook him for another seeker and smacked him with the flagpole.

"It's me, for God's sake. Is everyone all right?" he shouted to the people inside.

The door shot open, and Tom stood on the other side, brandishing the improvised weapon. "Everyone's fine. Are there any more of them?"

Oliver stood next to Anna and Asher by the back door of the hall and stared down into the snowy field below. The moonlight reflected off the snow, making it easy to see three figures breaking through the tree line, highlighted against the white backdrop.

"Guess they've figured out the barrier's broken," Anna said.

"The blood seekers are coming," Oliver turned toward Eric.

Eric stepped forward and looked down at the field. "How many?"

"Three that I can see, but there could be more," Oliver replied.

"Definitely more than three," Eric said, squinting at the field below.

Oliver took another look and saw the pack had grown to five or six. He swallowed hard. "How much ammunition do you have?"

"Two spare clips and what's left in this one."

"If the blood seekers get inside, they will kill everyone. The townspeople will have a much better chance if you stay with the gun. I don't know how many there will be, but all they'll have are knives and swords."

"What exactly are you suggesting?" Eric asked.

"I'll lead them away from the hall. I'll try to get them to the train station and Gideon." He paused. "Where's Madeline?"

"She went inside to find Martin," Eric replied.

"Perfect. She'll be better off staying behind with the rest of the town."

"I'm going with you," Anna said.

"Me too," Asher added.

Oliver looked at Asher, who had nothing but an empty flare gun. "How are you going to defend yourself?"

Asher lifted his shirt and pulled a leather-wrapped dagger from his belt. "Gideon gave this to me before we left. Guess he thought the flare gun might not be enough." He grinned.

"I can't let you go running off and getting yourself killed," Eric said.

"I'm not asking. The townspeople need you. Even if they get in, you've got your weapon. I don't know how many more are coming, and if they find out the townsfolk are hiding in the hall, you likely won't have enough bullets. Just lock the door, stay quiet, and don't open it until we get back."

Eric's eyebrows twitched, and Oliver assumed he was having a hard time taking orders, but his expression softened as he looked back at the people inside.

He turned toward the trio. "Just be careful."

"We will be back," Oliver added.

Eric patted him on the shoulder, and Oliver pushed the door closed.

"They're getting closer," Anna said, gripping her bat tightly.

The trio positioned themselves at the end of the dirt road, next to the marketplace.

The pack of blood seekers came into focus, six in total, led by a hulking beast. Oliver raised his weapon and prepared to fire. Once the seekers were close enough, he pulled the trigger, sending a bullet through the leader's left shoulder. He stumbled for a moment but regained his balance, grunting loudly as he ran toward them.

Oliver cocked again and fired, this time ignoring the giant in favor of one of the others flanking him. The bullet struck that seeker in the chest, and he fell, sliding in the snow.

"One down," Oliver said.

"At least we have their attention," Anna added.

As the trio sprinted toward the train station, Oliver struggled to reload his gun.

Gideon was watching from a distance, and by the time they'd reached the train, he had jumped down from the engine door and raised his sword, ready to strike.

The pack split in two, with the leader peeling off toward Gideon as the rest continued the chase.

As Oliver reached the side of the train, he twisted around and fired. The first shot missed completely, but the second struck one of the scrawnier blood seekers in the abdomen, sending him tumbling against a trash can.

"One for each of us!" Anna swung hard at an approaching blood seeker and knocked it back, but the creature quickly recovered.

Asher stood with dagger drawn, swiping wildly at another.

The third lunged at Oliver, who had no time to reload. The seeker brought his rusty sword down, but Oliver deflected with his weapon, which sent his gun sword flying down the station platform.

The seeker closed in and raised his sword once more. He grinned widely, flashing his broken yellow teeth.

As Oliver backed against the train, he remembered the lighter in his pocket—the magic left behind—and pulled the metal contraption free. He had no clue how to operate the device and no time to learn, but he flipped the lid and clicked the flint wheel as the others fought in his periphery.

A burst of flame shot from his palm, rushing from his hand and knocking him against the train. The fireball exploded off the seeker, who let out a bloody cry. Oliver screamed, too, because the flame had backfired, scorching his sleeve and burning his hand and lower arm.

The blood seeker writhed on the ground, rolling around in agony until he gradually came to rest, his burning body hissing in the snow.

Oliver turned toward the others and fired another incendiary burst at the seeker who had cornered Asher. The pain was more intense this time and radiated through his arm to the rest of his body.

Anna seemed to be holding her own, so Oliver set his sights on Gideon and the leader of the pack. The pain in his arm made focusing difficult, and Gideon was too close to his adversary for Oliver to send another clumsy burst of fire his way.

Although Gideon was tall and muscular, this seeker was more so, somehow thriving while the others had starved. He reflected every heavy blow Gideon delivered, and Gideon was slowing.

"There are more coming!" Anna yelled as she stood over a struggling blood seeker.

Oliver heard a predatory scream in the distance and broke into a cold sweat. *How many are there?*

Although Gideon's skirmish was blocking access to the engine and the first passenger car of the train for the time being, the door to the caboose sat exposed. Oliver hopped up on the metal step and unlocked the door.

"Get in!" he shouted to Asher. "We'll be right behind you. We won't be able to take all of them like this."

Asher hesitated.

"Just go!" Oliver shouted.

Asher climbed the steps into the caboose, and Oliver triggered the metal door behind him, sliding it into place.

"Get away from him!" Oliver shouted at Gideon.

The blood seeker swung, and Gideon stepped to one side, leaving enough room for another fireball. Oliver raised his aching hand and flicked the wheel, but the burst stopped short as the pain became too much to bear.

Gideon moved in to strike, but the creature delivered a swift kick to Gideon's chest, knocking him backward against a station bench. He then set his sights on Oliver, who tried to conjure another burst of fire with no luck. The fear of incinerating himself was all too real, and the pain made him shake. His mind raced to find a solution. As the seeker closed in, Oliver turned and sprinted toward the second train car, then he unlocked the door and climbed inside.

"Come and get me!" he yelled.

The plan was foolish, he was certain, but the seeker plodded after him, holding his makeshift blade ready to strike. He entered the car with the elaborate office and fish ponds then opened the door between his car and the caboose.

He waited for the blood seeker to follow him inside then shut the door as he hopped back down to the tracks.

As Gideon approached the door to the second car, Oliver shouted, "Wait!" He jumped in front of Gideon and pressed the button to close the exterior door, locking the blood seeker inside.

"He's trapped," he panted. "Not going to do any harm in there."

"They're coming," Anna said, looking toward the square.

Oliver fell to the ground as the pain in his arm pulsed.

"Are you all right?"

The train lurched forward on the tracks, its wet

joins squealing to life after days of sitting stationary in the Christchurch station.

"Where's the woman?" Oliver asked as his head spun. He had forgotten all about her during the fight. He rolled over toward the engine, but the door was shut. He caught his breath while he searched the horizon for additional blood seekers.

"We've got to get him to the train before the blood seekers get here," Anna told Gideon.

"No! What are you doing?" Oliver slurred.

Gideon lifted him by his shoulders as the train crept by.

"Let me go!" Oliver shouted but was too weak to fight Gideon off.

Anna hopped onto the end of caboose and helped Gideon lay Oliver on the caboose platform, tossing his gun blade next to him.

"Come on," Anna told Gideon.

Oliver lifted his head just in time to see Gideon leap from the end of the caboose back onto the station platform.

"What are you doing?" Anna shouted.

As the train pulled away, Gideon raced toward the town square, the direction of the blood seekers' howls.

Oliver's head fell backward against the metal grate as dizziness overcame him.

He looked into the sky, which flashed like a static

channel on an old television, shifting from overcast gray to light blue. He turned his head, and the snow seemed to wriggle on the ground, expanding and contracting, until it receded completely, replaced by green grass underneath. The signs of the storm that had ravaged Christchurch for several days disappeared in an instant, then Oliver's world went black.

CHAPTER TWELVE

Oliver awoke to Anna and Asher leaning over him. The ceiling of a train car had replaced the shifting sky.

"Feeling all right?" Asher asked.

Oliver rubbed his forehead. "I think so. How long was I out?"

"Just a few minutes," Anna replied. "Your face went pale, and you stopped responding. You must have gone into shock." She held up a vial of Asher's phosphorescent blood. "Fortunately, we found a few of these in the Collector's drawer."

Asher grinned. "I should start a business. I've seen the miracle cures on daytime TV. We would be rich."

A twinge of pain brought Oliver's attention to his arm. His sleeve had been burned, but his blistering red skin had mostly healed, and the last patch was bubbling as if insects were running underneath. Three empty vials lay on the floor next to him.

Anna and Asher helped Oliver sit up and leaned him against a wall.

Oliver looked around the room. The car must have served as both the Collector's sleeping quarters and his storage. A bed sat against the far wall, and stacks of wooden storage crates sat in one corner.

Oliver pushed himself to his feet and stumbled toward the blacked-out window. "Did you see the sky?"

"It flashed from gray to blue," Anna replied, "and Christchurch was back to normal by the time the train left town."

"That means Ruby's magic has to be on the train, right?" Oliver asked.

"We couldn't find anything in the car," Asher replied.

"If he's using her powers, do you think she's still alive?" Anna asked.

Asher lowered his head.

"Until we have proof otherwise, we assume she's alive," Oliver said. "Got it?"

Asher nodded.

Although Oliver was maintaining a calm facade, he had no clue about what awaited them at their destination. He'd wondered why Ruby had cut off all contact with them after promising to keep in touch. When she told him about magic left behind, she mentioned that Unnaturals had only so much to leave behind before having nothing left at all.

But what did she mean? Before they have no more power or no more life, period? And somehow, the storm projection seemed more powerful than what Ruby was capable of. She could pull off smaller illusions, but those tended to wipe her out. *How had the Collector pulled off something on such a massive scale?*

"I guess we'll just have to wait and see where this thing stops. Think he knows we're onboard?" Anna asked.

"I hope not. At least we don't have to worry about him finding us in this car, with that blood seeker between us." Oliver pulled the blackout curtain back from the window.

The train blazed down the tracks, and the lush greens of the countryside slowly shifted to a dingy palette of city grays. He recognized his old station as the Drury Street sign zipped by. Oliver hadn't been back to the city since his great escape to Christchurch more than a year prior.

"I wonder what the Collector's doing up there," Oliver said.

"Why don't you walk through the car next door and find out?" Anna asked. "Say hello to our friend on the way."

Oliver looked at the car door. "I could probably get a peek into the blood seeker's car, at least."

Anna's eyes widened.

"I'll take a look." He walked toward the metal door.

Oliver pressed the button to open the first door separating the two cars and stepped cautiously across the narrow metal platforms that served as an unsteady walkway between them. The small vent at the top of the next door provided just enough of a view of the office car. He stood up on his tiptoes and pressed his forehead against the metal slats.

The blood seeker was standing in the center of the room, staring blankly at the opposite metal wall as if locked in a trance. He swayed subtly as the train shifted, the edges of his tattered clothing rustling and his homemade sword dangling from his hand, scraping against the floor.

A metal ladder ran up the side of the car next to the door, and Oliver stepped back and placed his hand on a rung. *I could probably climb this. Maybe I can climb over and get a peek at the Collector.* He placed his foot on the bottom rung and looked down at the ground below. The train shifted violently, and he pivoted sideways.

No way.

"See anything?" Asher asked as Oliver reentered their car.

"Saw the blood seeker and found a ladder. No way I'm climbing it, though," he replied.

As they waited for the train to stop and the landscape shifted to countryside once more, Oliver practiced with the lighter on the rear platform of the caboose. He tried to avoid the bursts of flame that would leave him badly burned or tip off the Collector, and after a few fizzled starts, he sparked a few small fireballs that he held in his hand for a few seconds without burning his fingertips. The power seemed to be based on intent. When he fired at the blood seekers, he'd wanted them to die, and the lighter obliged, but the blowback had nearly killed him. Now, he was calmer and better able to control the flames.

Anna opened the door to the caboose and sat next to him as he conjured another fireball.

"That's cool," she said. "Getting the hang of it?"

"I think," he replied. "Seems like the bigger the flame, the more the damage to me."

Anna smirked.

"What? What could you possibly be smiling about?" Oliver asked.

She averted her eyes. "Nothing. It's silly, really, and definitely not the time to bring it up."

"Well, you'd better say it now. If he finds out we're on board, you may not have another chance."

"I was thinking of our first big honey harvest. You

wouldn't go near the hives. You were terrified, but not just of the hives—of everything. Now, look at you. If this is our last adventure, I'm just glad we get to have it together," she said. "I look back on what happened with the Siren a few months ago and think of how it might have ended. What if Simon had won? I would still be a mindless slave. At least this time, I can help." She looked up at him, and for a moment, her confident facade cracked.

"There's no one else in the world I'd rather have on my side when facing certain death," he said, "although you'd be a hell of a lot more helpful if you were three hundred pounds and could use a broadsword."

Anna laughed. "I came to tell you it looks like there's something up ahead. Come back inside."

Oliver extinguished the fireball and headed into the caboose.

The train crept through an abandoned industrial park. Rust ran down the sides of large holding tanks, intermingled among a complex series of pipes and concrete structures. Tall smokestacks sat derelict against the gray sky, some so tall they appeared to scrape the clouds.

A few dim yellow lights lit the track in front of them as the train lurched past a yard of junked freight cars.

Oliver imagined the place in full operation, with

thousands of factory workers flowing through the buildings, which produced God knew what, with steam puffing from the tall smokestacks like toxic cotton candy.

The train came to rest behind an old warehouse, its wheels screeching against the metal track, and the contents of the car shifted as it came to a stop. Wooden pallets filled a concrete slab behind the structure to capacity, stacked so high they teetered in the wind, leaving a curving path to a pair of industrial hangar doors.

The doors slowly slid apart as three muscular forms emerged from inside. Three henchman-looking types approached the engine.

Oliver checked the bullets in his weapon as Anna stared out at the men.

"How the hell are we supposed to navigate this place?" she asked.

The clunk of a metal train door echoed through the pallets as the Collector emerged from the engine, stepping down onto the concrete platform below. His angry red hair lay in a tangled mess, and he ran his fingers through it, revealing a long rip down one of his suit sleeves. He was shaking with fury.

"Get moving," he told the men. "There's a surprise for you in the next car. Might want to keep your distance. The gem is in the jar in my desk, but that thing in there nearly ripped my head off. Take care of it."

"I'll take the Collector, and you and Asher take the other three," Anna said.

Oliver looked over at her.

"What? Might as well get in a laugh or two before we go striding off toward our imminent doom."

Oliver crept to the outer door of the neighboring car and looked inside. The blood seeker was standing in the same place. As the train door slid open, the seeker twitched and seemed to snap out of a trance. He let out a low growl then a scream as he leapt through the car door, weapon ready.

The blood seeker's attack cut short a henchman's yelp. Screaming followed—then several gunshots, the flashes illuminating the inside of the office car. A sickening silence came next, and despite Oliver's strong desire to peek around the corner of the car, he remained still.

"The boss told him not to get too close," another henchman said. "Jesus... His blood's everywhere."

"Is he dead?" the other asked.

A single gunshot followed. "If he wasn't, he sure is now."

"What do you think was wrong with him? Rabies?"

"Don't matter now. Get the gem."

"What if there are more in there?"

"That's why you're going in first. Now, get going."

Oliver saw a henchman's shadow in the car entrance, and he ducked behind the door.

As the man rifled through the Collector's desk drawers, Oliver debated whether to attack. If he timed it right, he could slip in and dispatch the henchman, using his sword as a silent killer. He placed his hand on the door, looked down at his sword, and decided otherwise. *I've got no practice with the pointy end. What makes me think I can take him?*

The other man poked his head into the car. "Would you hurry? He's already in a shitty mood."

"Got it," the first replied.

Oliver recognized the specimen jar from The Parlor show, when Asher had suspended a row of them above the audience, each filled with a reanimated skeletal monkey. Although the blood remained, the monkey had been removed and replaced with a crystal.

"What's this thing supposed to do?" He shook the jar gently.

"It's none of our business."

"But—"

"We get paid to keep our questions to ourselves," the man replied.

Their boots clanked against the metal stairs as they stepped down onto the concrete platform.

"What about the other car?"

"We'll get it later. Better get this inside."

"You think this thing really has powers?"

"You saw what the bitch did—nearly gave Jimmy a heart attack."

Oliver clenched a fist.

"Ha! Might have been a better way to die than what just happened to him."

"He was a moron anyway. We're better off without him. Dunno why the boss kept him around. Let's go. The boss is gonna flip when he sees that new antique we got in. He's been chasing that thing for months."

As the men's footsteps clanked away, Oliver poked his head around the edge of the car. Two bloody forms lay splayed on the concrete—one the massive blood seeker, the other obviously Jimmy, who looked to be in pieces.

Oliver opened the door to the caboose and joined the other two inside.

"They took a crystal out of the Collector's office, and it's stored in Asher's blood. That must be how it can produce such a powerful illusion." He traced the outline of the lighter in his pocket. "I think the lighter must feed on me for power, but the blood must fuel the gem."

Anna opened her mouth to speak but had trouble coming up with a response.

"I know it sounds crazy, but at this point,

anything's possible, right? And at least the blood seeker and one of the Collector's thugs are out of the way," Oliver said.

"They've got guns," Anna said. "How are we going to get in without getting shot?"

Oliver pulled the lighter from his pocket. "At least we've got this and a few vials of blood in case anything goes wrong. Maybe we should wait a while until things settle down then sneak in to try to find Ruby. We'll get through this."

"Look," Anna whispered, pointing toward the window above their heads.

Oliver stuck his head over the edge of the ledge and looked out into the concrete yard. The two remaining henchmen were approaching the train once more.

"They're coming toward us," she said.

Oliver's heart dropped. He pointed at the door at the end of the caboose. "We've got to go now." He rushed toward the back and pressed the button to open the door. "Come on."

They slipped out onto the caboose platform, and Oliver closed the door. As that latch clicked, the side door opened.

They ducked under the window and lowered themselves down onto the tracks. Oliver peered underneath the car to look for the henchmen's feet, and once he saw the coast was clear, they darted behind a few stacks of pallets.

Through the slats of a pallet, Oliver watched the men unload the caboose, removing the Collector's belongings and carrying them back toward the warehouse.

Oliver motioned for Anna and Asher to follow, and they slipped between stacks of pallets toward the back of the warehouse.

They slid along the side of the building, careful to remain hidden, until Oliver noticed an old plate-glass basement window near his foot. He knelt to look inside and found a row of large circular chambers outlined by the red glow of an Exit sign.

"It's the boiler room," Anna whispered next to him.

He scanned the room for any activity then pushed on the rusted metal frame. After a few firm shoves, the top of the window popped out toward them.

"Think we can fit?" she asked.

Oliver turned around and tucked his feet through the gap in the window. His feet searched for something on which to stand but found nothing but empty space. As he leapt down to the basement floor, he cracked his head on the top of the window. Gritting his teeth, he grabbed the back of his head, holding in a cry of pain.

He searched the room and found an old step stool, which he placed under the window for Anna. He guided her down, and her descent was much more elegant than his. Asher followed.

"You all right?" she asked.

Oliver nodded.

As their eyes adjusted, Oliver crossed the room to a workbench. He rummaged through a pile of old tools and knelt to search the shelf underneath.

"What are you looking for?" she whispered with an air of desperation.

Oliver emerged with a long silver flashlight. "Just in case," he replied.

They crept out into the hallway, and Oliver stood for a moment, listening for footsteps.

The air was moist, and the plink of water droplets echoed through the hallway.

Oliver clicked the switch on the flashlight, but nothing happened at first. After a few smacks against his wrist, a dingy yellow beam illuminated the hallway. They walked down the corridor, passing several storage rooms before coming to an old concrete staircase.

Moisture stained the walls there, brown streaks running down the chipped gray paint. At the top of the stairs, a heavy metal door blocked their path into the main part of the warehouse, but a light shone through the frosted glass.

Oliver flipped the flashlight off, pulled his weapon from its holster, then slid the flashlight into its place.

He clicked one hilt hammer back on his weapon while he gripped the lighter tightly in the other hand. After pulling the door open slowly, he peered around the corner. Another hallway greeted them, stacked with cardboard boxes and old office equipment.

He gestured for Anna and Asher to follow as he made his way down the hall.

The light was coming from a door at the end of the hallway, and Oliver braced himself for confrontation on the other side.

"Ready?" he whispered.

Anna raised her bat, and Asher stood behind her with his dagger drawn.

The door sat ajar, and Oliver aimed the blade of his gun sword through the crack. He grabbed the handle and pushed the door open, rapidly scanning the room as the sword followed his gaze.

Like the hallway, the room was lined with cardboard boxes and old equipment, but the center of the room housed an old metal gurney that had a woman strapped to it.

CHAPTER THIRTEEN

A brown burlap sack covered the woman's face, but Oliver recognized the black curls sticking out from underneath, and the tattoos were the dead giveaway. Her slender arms were covered with what looked like cigarette burns.

Oliver held his breath as he slowly lifted the bag, hoping to find her alive. The eyes that met his took his breath away.

Oliver barely recognized Ruby's sunken face. She squinted at first, overcome by the bright light. When her pupils adjusted, tears formed in the corners of her eyes.

"Where's Asher?" Her hoarse voice sounded as though she hadn't spoken in days.

Asher stepped forward and leaned over the table, holding his hand to his mouth as he scanned Ruby's emaciated form. She tried to reach for him, but a leather strap held her tight to the gurney. So he slid a shaking hand under hers and squeezed. Then Asher wiggled the strap free, loosening its grip on her wrist.

"We're going to get you out of here," he said, his voice wavering.

Oliver and Asher loosened the remaining straps, and she rubbed her wrists, which had become red from the restraints.

"I told them I couldn't give any more," she said. "They took it all—locked it all away in that damned stone." She looked up at Oliver. "What did he do with it?"

"The gem's in the warehouse," Oliver replied. "He used it to trap Christchurch in a fake blizzard. We chased him back here."

Ruby's breath quickened, and she grabbed Asher's hand. "You shouldn't be here. If he gets to you, he'll use you like he used me."

"It's okay," Asher replied, rubbing her gently on the back. "He may have the gem, but we've got his firepower. We came to rescue you."

"Do you hear that?" Anna whispered. "Sounds like someone's coming."

Ruby's eyes narrowed. She looked at the dagger dangling in Asher's hand and pointed. "Give me that and strap my legs back in."

"What? Why?" Asher asked.

"Just do it."

Oliver strapped Ruby's legs back to the gurney, and Asher handed Ruby his weapon. She slid the dagger underneath her right forearm, and Asher laid the straps loose across her wrists to give the appearance that they were still restraining her.

"Hide," she said through gritted teeth.

Footsteps echoed through the hallway as Oliver, Anna, and Asher hid behind a large stack of filing boxes. Oliver positioned himself so that he had a clear view of the metal table.

As one of the henchmen entered the room, Oliver noticed the burlap sack on the ground, but they had no time to put it back in place.

"Now, how the hell did you get the bag off?" the man asked as he approached. He walked over and picked it up then leaned down to put it back on Ruby.

The strike was almost too fast to see as Ruby swiped the dagger across the man's front. He opened his mouth to scream, but the only sound that emerged was a desperate gargle. Ruby loosened her other restraint and sat up on the table.

"You should have killed me when you had the opportunity," she said.

The man fell to the floor, still struggling. After a few more agonized coughs, he stopped moving, and his arms fell limp to his sides, revealing his bloodstained shirt underneath.

Ruby loosened her foot straps and called for the others. Oliver was too stunned to move.

"One down. How many more to go?" she asked as she wiped the blood off the dagger and handed it back to Anna, who looked as though she was about to vomit.

"He had it coming," Ruby said. "Now, help me down." She held up her burn-spotted arms.

Oliver and Asher helped her off the table, but her legs fell out from under her as soon as her feet hit the floor.

She grunted in frustration as she tried to push herself back up.

"Why *didn't* he kill you when he had the chance?" Oliver asked.

"They wanted to see if the magic would regenerate on its own." She pushed up off the ground and, with Oliver and Asher bracing her, balanced herself. She resembled a newborn fawn just learning to walk, legs wobbling as she took a few cautious steps.

"They were using me as a guinea pig—give me a little time to recover then try to squeeze more power out of me. That way, they'd have a better understanding of how it worked."

"Did it come back?" Oliver asked. "Your power, I mean."

"Does it look like it came back?" she spat. Then her gaze softened. "I'm sorry. No. I heard them talking. If it didn't work, they were going to try Asher's blood on me. They must still have a supply from The Parlor."

"They put the gem in one of the monkey jars from the show and fueled it with Asher's blood. Something about it gave the gem enough power to cast an illusion over the entire town."

"Near immortality and infinite power—no wonder he's so hell-bent on getting Asher," Anna said. "Let's get out of here."

"How will we get home? We can't turn the train around. We're in the middle of an industrial park," Oliver replied.

"There have to be cars around, right? How else would they have gotten here?" Asher approached the body of the fallen henchman and checked his pockets. "See?" He held up a key chain with a car key dangling on the end.

"If we let the Collector weasel out of this, he'll be back, and we might not be so lucky next time. We have to find him and make sure he doesn't walk away free." Oliver pulled the lighter from his pocket. "We've got real fire. All the Collector has are illusions."

"And probably guns," Anna added. "And the last time you used that thing to defend yourself, you set your arm on fire and went into shock."

He patted his pocket. "I still have a few vials of blood, just in case, but I think I've got a better grip on how it works. And maybe we could solve two problems at once, but it means we'd have to split up. If you and I go find the Collector, Asher and Ruby can go find our getaway vehicle."

Asher's eyes widened. "We can't leave you."

"I think he's right," Anna replied. "It's foolish for all of us to go together, especially with Ruby in the state she's in."

"I can hear you, you know." Ruby gestured for Oliver and Asher to let go, and she took a few more practice steps across the room. "Do I need to remind you what I did with the dagger?" She gestured toward the man on the floor.

"It's a good plan," Oliver replied. "If things go poorly, at least we've got a shot at getting away if the car's out front."

"Feel up to driving?" Asher asked Ruby. "I've never done it before."

"I may be weak, but I'm not an invalid." She smirked.

"Ruby can keep the dagger. Just give me something blunt, and I'll come out swinging." Asher scanned the room and picked up an old metal pipe from a stack in the corner of the room.

"Sure you want to come with me?" Oliver asked Anna.

"We beat the Witch together, and we can do the same with the Collector," she replied.

"Are you sure?" he asked.

She looked up at him. "Without a doubt."

They entered the hallway and walked back toward the basement staircase.

"There's an open window in the boiler room," Asher said. "We should be able to climb out into the back storage yard." He turned to Oliver. "We'll meet you out front."

"If we're not out by sunrise or someone else finds you, leave without us," Oliver replied.

Asher hesitated.

"Better that two of us get out alive than none of us," Oliver said.

Asher nodded. "Be careful."

After a few goodbyes, Asher and Ruby descended the staircase to the boiler room.

Oliver and Anna stood for a moment, just the two of them in the desolate hallway filled with boxes and old junk.

Oliver handed Anna his gun blade. "Take this." He unstrapped its leather belt and gave it to her. "Just click a hammer back and aim it at the thing you want to die.

If that fails, stab them with the pointy end." He smirked.

"What about you?"

"The lighter should be more than enough."

"I hope you're right," Anna said as they walked down the hallway.

"Right about what?"

"That we'll get through this," she said.

The hallway led to the main warehouse, dumping them out along the front wall of the massive room. Oliver listened intently, but the place was quiet, aside from a mechanical hum vibrating through the building.

Several crates hid them from view as they crept along the wall under a tall set of stairs leading to a mezzanine level.

Oliver squeezed between two of the crates to get a look into the main room. Tall industrial warehouse shelves lined the room, stretching up to the metal roof. Heavy-looking crates lined some shelves, while others held filing boxes stacked atop each other.

The door at the top of the steps squealed open, and Oliver pressed himself against the wall underneath.

"I don't know what he's doing. The lazy idiot's probably off napping again. I'll go find him." The henchman's boots clanged against the metal stairs as he descended.

Although Oliver doubted he'd be heard over the

warehouse's industrial white noise, he held his breath and watched through the slits in the metal steps. When the henchman reached the concrete floor, he walked in front of the crates and toward the hallway from which Oliver and Anna had come.

Oliver wasn't sure what to do. Burning the man alive seemed too brutal of a punishment although Ruby had surprised them all with her use of the dagger.

Once the man passed through the door to the hallway, Oliver gestured for Anna to follow. He crept toward the doorway and peered inside. *He's going to find the body.* Oliver's pulse quickened. Figuring two sets of feet would be more easily detected than one, he gestured for Anna to wait at the end of the hallway.

Oliver noticed an old caster sitting atop a stack of cardboard boxes. He picked it up quietly and held in a yelp as the rough edge of the metal wheel sent a jagged splinter into his index finger.

The man turned toward the closed door of the room that once held Ruby strapped to the gurney. They hadn't bothered to hide the body, which lay slumped next to it.

As the man opened the door, Oliver rushed in on his tiptoes.

"Jesus," the man said.

Before he could reach the body, Oliver cracked him in the head with the heavy wheel. The henchman toppled like a bowling pin, falling face-first onto the floor.

Anna ran down the hall to help.

"Help me get him onto the gurney," he said.

They dragged the man by his arms and lifted him onto the table with a clumsy heave. They strapped his arms and legs tightly, and Oliver found an old rag to serve as an impromptu gag.

Anna stood back. "Is he dead? He's not moving."

Oliver noticed the subtle rise and fall of the man's chest. "No, see?" He pointed. "Thank God."

They crept down the hallway and back toward the main warehouse. As Oliver rounded the staircase, Anna followed closely behind. They reached the halfway point, but as the staircase turned in the other direction, the Collector was standing there, waiting for them.

"Brave of you to follow me here. Foolish, but brave." He rested one hand on the metal railing and held the jar containing the crystal in the other.

"I much prefer the lighter," he said. "This... Well, I still don't quite understand how it works. Fire is simple. Point and shoot." He laughed and made a finger gun, firing it in Oliver's direction. "Don't even have to have good aim."

"It isn't yours to use," Oliver said. "It belongs to Ruby."

"Oh, how rude of me. I suggest you come up and take it, then," he said with a wide grin.

"Your men are dead. There's no one left to protect you."

"Those men were overpaid anyway." He held the specimen jar in his hands, and the gem bounced against the glass. "This is all I need. A world full of special abilities, and all I'm gifted with is a wimpy alter ego. But this changes things."

The Collector stared into the gem, and the stairs beneath Oliver's feet shifted. He and Anna grabbed the railing and stumbled down to the concrete floor.

Once Oliver had regained his balance, he looked up at the Collector, on the mezzanine. "There's a big difference between the magic in the gem and the magic in the lighter."

"Oh?" The Collector feigned surprise.

"What the lighter can do is real." Oliver pulled it from his pocket and held it up.

The Collector hid his surprise behind a scoff. "So you found it. Thanks for bringing it back to me."

He raised an arm and aimed toward the metal roof. The water pipes overhead pulled loose from the ceiling and slithered like large metal snakes, spewing water from their mouths.

Anna turned to run, but Oliver grabbed her by the arm.

"Parlor tricks, remember?" he said. He stood his ground as the pipes descended.

Anna gripped his shoulder, her fingers trembling, and he flicked the flint wheel and sent a short burst of flame in the Collector's direction. His hand burned, but the pain stopped at his wrist.

The crash of glass was followed by a shout from the top of the mezzanine, and the ceiling and pipes of the building had returned to their proper places.

As flames consumed the room at the top of the stairs, iridescent blood poured out the doorway and through the metal floor grates of the mezzanine, running down the wall in long glowing streaks.

The Collector rushed inside. His screams weren't those of pain—he was angry. Flames licked the edges of the broken office window as they spread deeper inside. Plumes of fire-extinguisher smoke billowed out the broken window as the Collector tried to control the fire inside.

"What have you done?" he yelled, emerging from the staircase with the specimen jar tucked under one arm and a staff in the other hand.

The man descended the long metal staircase, stopped midway, and set the jar down.

"Haven't had time to practice with this one, but I

think you'll enjoy it. I was hoping to keep my warehouse in one piece, but you're not giving me much of a choice," the Collector said as he raised the staff.

"Oliver!" Anna shouted as she pointed at the ceiling above him.

An industrial ceiling fan came crashing down.

This isn't an illusion.

Oliver rolled to one side as a blade narrowly missed his leg.

The storage shelves around them tumbled, cascading toward them like rows of falling dominoes, with the sound of heavy metal and wooden crates crashing into heaps of twisted metal and debris. He and Anna raced toward the front of the room. The Collector had fallen backward against the wall, seemingly overcome by the blowback from the staff.

As they dodged the last of the falling shelves, Oliver prepared to strike again. He lifted his hand and put his thumb to the flint wheel, but his hand froze, paralyzed by some invisible force.

The Collector leaned against the railing and trembled as he lifted Oliver from the ground with his telekinetic grip. "I'll tear you apart!" he screamed.

Oliver felt the invisible force tugging his limbs in opposite directions. Just as he was sure his wrist would pop, a shot rang out from below, breaking the Collector's concentration and releasing Oliver.

As Oliver fell, he let out a clumsy burst of flame from his fingertips.

The Collector dodged but fell headfirst down the second half of the metal staircase, tumbling until he came to rest on the concrete floor.

Oliver landed hard and rolled an ankle.

The burst ignited a puddle of grease under the staircase and sped to a nearby shelf. The flames quickly climbed to stacks of boxes and crates.

"We've got to get out of here," Anna said as she tucked the smoking gun blade under her arm and helped Oliver to his feet.

The Collector's form lay obscured by flame and smoke, but Oliver couldn't bring himself to leave the man—or, more importantly, the innocent woman deep down inside.

"We can't just let him die here." He pressed a sleeve up against his mouth, trying to filter out the smoke, but his eyes still stung.

As they passed the staircase, Oliver noticed the crumpled form on the floor. The Collector had been replaced, once again, by the woman, collapsed against a steel beam.

"Help me!" he shouted.

He knelt next to the woman and shook her, trying to wake her. She lay limp, so he slapped her lightly on a cheek.

"Hey, come on," he said. "We gotta go."

She jerked awake and looked around the room as though seeing it for the first time.

"We have to go," he repeated in loud staccato syllables.

He and Anna propped her up until she recovered enough to walk on her own.

"I have to find the gem," Oliver said.

He left Anna with the woman while he searched the stairs.

In the blast's chaos, the specimen jar must have fallen from the stairs and shattered on the floor, leaving splatters of blood and broken glass where it fell. Fortunately, the gem remained intact.

They led the woman through the warehouse toward the large doors on the other side, but a wall of flame stood in their way. So they turned toward the door under the stairs of the mezzanine, where they had ambushed one of the henchmen.

They passed into the hallway, but smoke had formed a wall of black as it billowed through the doorway.

They rushed down the hall until they came to the room with the metal gurney. As soon as the man strapped to the table saw them, he began cursing and struggling to pull himself free.

As Oliver grabbed the metal handle next to the

man's head, the man spat in Oliver's direction. "I'll kill you when I get out of this," he said.

Oliver let go of the gurney. "I can leave you here if you'd prefer."

The man laid his head back on the metal table. "No, take me with you."

"Thought so," Oliver said. "Is there another way out of here?"

"Down the hallway next to the basement door. That'll lead you to the front."

"Perfect," Oliver replied.

He and Anna pushed the gurney down the hall, toward the front of the building, while the woman followed close behind.

When they reached the front door, the woman tugged at Oliver's arm. He tried to guide her through, but she pulled away.

"What are you doing? Come on!" he shouted.

"He'll just come back. He always comes back," she said, stepping back into the building.

"There are people who can help you. *We* can help you."

"They've tried to help me," she said, tears streaking her soot-covered face. "He'll win, and this is the only way I can stop him for good." She stepped farther back into the building.

"No!" Oliver shouted as he reached out for her.

"It's better this way." Before Oliver could stop her, she slammed the door and ran down the hall toward the blaze. He watched her through the window as she disappeared into the wall of smoke.

"We have to go," Anna said.

"We can't leave her!" He gripped the door handle and yanked, but the door was locked tight.

"It's too late for her."

The fire reached the hallway and worked its way along the walls.

"We can't save her!" Anna shouted.

Her words pulled Oliver out of his temporary daze.

"Let's go." He hobbled toward the front steps, towing the gurney and letting it bounce awkwardly down the stairs.

Ruby and Asher were waiting on the crumbled asphalt road in front of the building, leaning against an old compact car and visibly shaken by the conflagration.

"Are you all right?" Ruby asked as she rushed over.

"Fine," Oliver replied.

They stood in front of the mammoth warehouse and watched the building burn as Oliver pulled a vial from his pocket and poured it over his burned hand.

Oliver handed the gem to Ruby. "I think this belongs to you."

Ruby's eyes glistened in the firelight. "You found

it." She flipped the gem over in her hand then set it on the ground.

"What are you doing?" Oliver asked.

"Help me find a rock," she replied.

Oliver obliged and found a broken chunk of concrete sitting next to the warehouse steps.

Ruby knelt and held out her hand for the concrete. She struggled to lift it over her head, focusing on the gem.

"Do you need help?" he asked.

"I have to do it," she replied.

The first swing was a miss as she struck the edge of the gem and sent it skittering across the pavement. After she sighed and shuffled over, she lifted the rock once more and brought it down square in the center of the clear stone, cracking its surface. Light beams broke through the crack, reminding Oliver of the Briarwood barrier breaking. She lifted the chunk of concrete a final time and brought it down hard, shattering the stone. A burst of light consumed her, illuminating her pale form while somehow failing to spread to her surroundings.

As the others stood and watched, she breathed deeply, each breath drawing more light into her body until little remained but a faint afterglow.

"This feels amazing!" she said, still glowing like the

luminescent Santa Izzy had placed in the yard the year before.

They watched as the fire reached the pallets in the back of the warehouse and towering flames licked the sky.

The blare of sirens echoed through the industrial park.

"We better get out of here," Oliver said.

Ruby walked to the driver's side of the car and hopped inside.

"So what do we do with him?" Asher pointed at the henchman still strapped to the gurney.

"Let the police find him," Oliver replied.

As they drove down the windy drive, the car backfiring once or twice along the way, Oliver looked into the rearview mirror as the building burned behind him. When they reached the main road and the first signs of civilization, a fire truck raced past toward the flaming building.

CHAPTER FOURTEEN

The sun rose as the stolen car sputtered into Christchurch. Oliver parked next to the town hall and scanned the horizon for roaming blood seekers.

The bodies of two seekers lay in the stone walkway to the hall's front entrance. The doors were still locked tight, so Oliver pounded hard on one with his fist.

"Who's there?" The voice on the other side sounded like Martin's.

"Oliver," he replied.

"Oh, thank God."

Gideon was the first to stick his head out, sword still clenched in a fist, prepared for any surprises. When he saw Oliver, his expression softened, and he opened the door wide.

The townsfolk inside rushed toward them.

Oliver spotted Eric in the crowd as he approached. "We still have work to do," he said. "Blood seekers are still running around Briarwood, and we have to find Izzy. The train is gone, so you shouldn't have any trouble calling the station in Amberley."

"So the storm was just a trick?" Eric asked.

"Just an illusion," Oliver replied.

"What happened to the woman?" Eric asked.

Oliver lowered his head. "She and the Collector are both dead. We've got to get back to get Izzy and take care of the remaining blood seekers."

"You should let the police handle it. Once we get more people over here—"

"You've seen what the seekers are capable of. Do you really want to send a bunch of officers into the woods?" Oliver asked. "They may have guns, but the seekers are wild animals. We've got more than enough firepower, and we know the town layout. We can take care of them."

Eric rubbed his temples. "You haven't steered me wrong so far. Just go before I change my mind."

"I'm coming with you," Ruby said. "Should be of some use to you now that I've gotten my power back."

Oliver turned to Asher.

"I know, I know—I'll stay here where it's safe."

"No," Oliver replied. "I was going to say we should all go together."

Asher grinned.

Oliver made one final march to Briarwood with Ruby, Anna, Asher, and Gideon close at his side. Gideon seemed eager to get back, his hands fiddling with the wrappings on the hilt of his sword.

"I'm sure they're okay," Oliver said.

As they approached the center of town, the bodies of several blood seekers lay scattered throughout the square, arrows lying haphazardly next to them.

"Aymes must have been practicing his aim." Oliver traced the edge of the town hall up to the metal lantern and saw the archer perched in the shattered window frame.

When he saw the group, he jumped from his seat and waved his bow enthusiastically.

"Praise be!" he yelled. "I was starting to think you'd all been slaughtered. Is the Collector dead?"

"Roasted!" Oliver shouted back. He felt a twinge of sadness when he thought of the woman running back into the blaze. "We came to help clear the town of blood seekers."

Aymes gestured for them to come inside. Oliver's ankle throbbed as they approached the side door. The long walk through the woods had taken its toll on him.

After a few knocks on the wooden door, the viewing window slid open, revealing the Clockmaker's wild eyebrows and smiling eyes on the other side.

The reinforcement bar fell to the floor, and the Clockmaker opened the door. "So good to see you!" As they entered, he looked at Ruby. "Who is your friend?"

"My name's Ruby," she replied as she looked around the workroom.

"Nice to meet you, Ruby," he replied. "Izzy is waiting upstairs for you with the others."

He led them to the entrance of the main hall and pulled the heavy doors open.

Oliver scanned the room for Izzy. Pan lay cuddled against her as both napped in the corner of the room, and Nekko gnawed on a piece of straw nearby, clearly unhappy with her Briarwood diet.

"Izzy!" he shouted.

Izzy jolted awake. Pieces of straw stuck in her hair as she stood and rushed toward them, Pan close behind.

"You made it," she said, tears welling in her eyes. "I was so worried." She tried to hug Oliver, Anna, and Asher at once, but her reach was too narrow, so she settled for one at a time.

"The Collector is dead, but we've still got to clear the rest of the blood seekers from town," Oliver said.

Izzy looked at Ruby. "Wasn't sure I'd ever see you again," Izzy said.

"She's been preoccupied," Oliver said. "But we

need to get to Aymes and clear out the town before the police get here and start snooping around."

"I guess I'll just return to the hay then," Izzy replied. "It's actually quite comfortable once you bunch it up the right way."

They reached the platform and the empty blood pool above the atrium.

"Asher's told me about this place, at least the bits and pieces he could remember, but words don't do it justice," Ruby said, admiring the copper door as they passed through.

Aymes stood from his perch in front of the window. Gideon approached, and the two slapped each other's shoulders in a manly embrace.

"Good to see you, my friend," Aymes said.

"We've come back to kill the rest of the blood seekers," Oliver said.

"And how do you plan to destroy them? With that puny little explosive sword of yours?"

Oliver pulled the Collector's lighter from his pocket. "The Collector's power wasn't his own." He flicked the lighter and formed a small fireball in his hand. "I'm sure we can destroy the blood seekers with it." Although he was better able to control the flame, Oliver was running out of blood vials to heal himself from the inevitable burns. He only hoped they'd last until the group cleared the town.

Aymes backed toward the window. "So we're resorting to dark magic, then? What about her?" Aymes pointed at Ruby. "She a witch too?"

Ruby lifted her arm and pointed her hand toward the broken window. The jagged edges of broken glass shifted, forming razor-like teeth held together by the corroded copper frame. The archer stepped back into the room as the giant metal maw snapped shut around him, enclosing him in a mouth made of metal and glass.

"Still don't think women can help?" Anna asked.

"Let me out!" Aymes shouted as he cowered in his imaginary cage.

"Keep him in there for a minute." Anna grinned.

"Well, are we going to clear the town of blood seekers or stand here?" Asher asked.

"I've been wondering the same thing," Ruby replied.

She seemed enamored with her surroundings. Had the situation been different, this would have been the perfect place to come to find odd trinkets for The Parlor.

* * *

OLIVER HAD BEEN QUITE frightened of the blood seekers before, but the power of the lighter surged through him, begging to be used. Oliver, Aymes, Gideon, and Ruby moved from building to building, searching for blood seekers and dispatching them along the way. Bursts of flame shot between the trees as they approached the back end of Briarwood. Now and then, when the burns became too much to bear, Oliver would stop to apply a vial of blood to his singed skin. He did his best to leave the buildings intact, allowing the others to dispatch those few seekers found indoors. He thought of Izzy's home, now a pile of ash. He wanted to ensure those in the hall had homes to return to, if only temporarily. They had been through enough. When the group had trouble luring them from the buildings, Ruby would draw the seekers out with an illusion.

Aymes had been right—most of the seekers had scattered to the back end of Briarwood, shifting to a large barn next to the forest when their source of human nourishment had dwindled.

A small farm cottage sat beside the large barn.

"Shall we go inside?" Oliver asked.

"Burn it," Aymes replied.

"What about the house?" Oliver asked.

"Both are mine. Burn them," he said once more.

Aymes turned his back while Oliver swept his hand back and forth, flames spewing out and over-taking the wooden structures. As the barn caught, two or three blood seekers pushed through the flames and out the large barn door.

Before Oliver could call Aymes's attention to them, Gideon tapped the archer on the shoulder. Oliver watched Aymes's face as he downed the blood seekers. He wondered if the man had had a family but quickly ushered the thought from his mind.

When they returned to the hall, Oliver saw flashing lights at the top of the hill. Several figures waited in the distance, leaning against police cruisers. Eric must have told them to hold off, to give Oliver a chance to take care of things.

Oliver thought for a moment, looking at the hulking figure of Gideon with his broadsword.

"The police will take this place over," he said.

"Who?" Aymes asked.

They have no idea who police are.

"Men who enforce the law. Now that the barrier is broken, they will find the town hall and may take the people inside."

Aymes tightened his grip on his bow. "Then we will kill them before they have the chance."

"No, they are here to help you. They will ensure your people's safety."

"Why should we trust the outsiders?"

Oliver massaged his temples. "I'm an outsider...

Look, we don't have time to debate this. Trust me. And you have to hide your weapons."

Aymes scoffed.

"Blend in with the other townspeople. Let them find you in the hall. If you have weapons, it will only lead to more questions and make you look responsible for all the violence. You'll be lumped in with the blood seekers."

Aymes looked at Gideon.

Gideon patted Oliver on the shoulder and nodded.

"Modern life isn't so bad," Ruby added, "medicine, reliable food, and a definite lack of bloodthirsty creatures."

Gideon dropped his broadsword on the ground and gestured for Aymes to do the same with his bow. Aymes reluctantly set his bow down and unslung the quiver from his shoulder.

As they reached the hall, Oliver ushered Gideon and Aymes inside. "We'll shut you in here and let them discover you. Just pretend you've been locked away," he said.

As Gideon turned toward the people inside the hall, Oliver grabbed his arm.

Gideon turned toward him, and they locked eyes.

"Thank you for all you've done," Oliver said. "I'm sorry about Mercy. I wish we could have saved her."

Gideon looked at the floor.

"Once you're out of here, come find us. Not sure what's next, now that Izzy's house is gone, but we'll have a place for you. You're family. The same goes for Aymes and Clockmaker."

Gideon looked up from the ground, eyes red but refusing to shed tears. He grabbed Oliver by his shoulder and pulled him in for a rugged warrior hug.

After Izzy and Anna corralled Pan and Nekko, Oliver and Ruby barricaded the door into the meeting hall.

The group reached the town square, and Oliver turned back to take one last look at Briarwood's hall. He wasn't sure if he'd ever return since Izzy's house had been destroyed or if he'd ever see any of his Briarwood comrades again.

They broke through the tree line to the field downhill from Izzy's.

"Do you think the police will take the town?" Asher asked.

"Bodies are scattered everywhere—they'd have to at least question the townspeople," Anna replied.

"Do you think they'll let them go back to Briarwood?"

No one seemed to know how to answer. Even if the citizens could return, Oliver was certain the town wouldn't be permitted to continue as it had, outside the rule of law. And with many townspeople killed and resources destroyed, Briarwood's remaining self-suffi-cient would be difficult.

The sight must have been strange for the police officers to behold—five humans, a feline, and a corgi pup ascending the hill into Christchurch square.

Will rounded his police cruiser. "Are you all right?" he asked.

"Just a few bumps," Oliver replied.

"Wasn't sure how much longer I could keep the others from stumbling down this way. Eric sent me down here to keep an eye out."

"Are these Amberley officers?"

"Amberley, Circleville—half the damned state's mulling around or on its way."

Will gestured for them to enter the cruiser. "Come on, I'll take you to the police station. Eric's waiting for you."

They crammed into the vehicle, a feat in itself with five adventurers and two animals, and headed toward the police station, which was abuzz with activity.

Eric stood talking to another officer—one who appeared to be much higher in the chain of command, based on appearance and demeanor. Eric looked toward them as they entered. "If this isn't déjà vu..." he said as he rushed over. "Do what you need to do?" he asked under his breath.

Oliver nodded. "The townspeople are in the hall. Make sure they're taken care of."

"Will mentioned seeing fire down the hill. Want to tell me what that's all about?"

Oliver grinned. "The job's done. What more do you need to know?"

CHAPTER FIFTEEN

Oliver awoke to corgi feet shuffling around his head. He stretched his back and cracked his neck, trying to ease a large crick that had formed at its base. Asher was snoozing on the couch next to him, and Pan licked his hand, which hung slack over the edge of the couch.

The cottage had been quiet, for such a tiny house packed with so many people. Oliver wrapped the blanket he'd been using around his shoulders and walked to the kitchen in search of a caffeine source. He spotted a coffee pot and a bag of beans in the corner next to the sink, and as he grabbed the pot to fill it with fresh water, he noticed Izzy sitting on one of the wooden lounge chairs outside.

"Aren't you freezing out here?" he asked, poking his head out the back door.

"Oh, it's not that bad," she replied, patting the chair next to her. "Come sit for a minute."

Oliver pulled the blanket tight and sat.

"What are you doing out here?"

"Just watching the waves." Izzy rubbed her lips with her index finger.

The crisp breeze created ripples that stretched across the lake. The ducks had flown south for the winter, and most of the fish lay dormant at the bottom, pacified by the frigid water.

"How are you holding up?" he asked.

"It will take me a while to get over this one, kiddo. Just happy we all made it out alive—that's what really matters."

"Ruby says we could stay with her at The Parlor," Oliver replied. "Think she's looking for some company, now she's decided to go back to Amberley. She'll also need help to clean up the place."

"That's kind of her," Izzy replied. "You know, Madeline offered us the same? Said we could stay with her as long as we need. Can you imagine? A year ago, that woman wouldn't be caught dead with me, and now she's offering to let us move in."

"This town cares about you, Izzy."

"We'll need to stay somewhere until the insurance check clears—thank God for that."

"Think you'll rebuild there?"

"Dunno. Everything happens for a reason—perhaps this is the cosmos's way of telling us it's time to try something new," she replied.

"At least we still have the bakery and the hives," Oliver said.

Asher stuck his face out through the crack in the back door.

"Anna's making breakfast. She wanted to know how pancakes sound."

"Delightful," Izzy replied. "We'll be in in a minute."

"Better hurry—you'll freeze out here."

"Why does everyone keep saying that? It's not that cold," she replied.

Asher rubbed his arms as he closed the door and returned to the kitchen.

"It *is* supposed to snow again this weekend," Oliver said. "Not quite a hallucinatory apocalyptic blizzard like this week, but snow all the same."

"Bring it on," Izzy replied.

Oliver looked out over the lake and recalled his conversation with Anna on the roof of The Horseman, more than a year prior. She would sit out back, look at the lake, and imagine she was somewhere else, maybe on the coast of an exotic country, anywhere but Christchurch. Looking back over his shoulder through the kitchen window and seeing Anna standing at the sink, he wondered if she still felt the same.

Oliver felt different about Christchurch now. Originally, the town had been an escape for him, a place to hide from responsibilities he didn't care to face. But the more he'd gotten to know the town and the people in it, the more he realized the place wasn't just an escape. Despite the challenges, the deaths, and the destruction he'd faced, all because of an invisible town on the other side of the woods, he couldn't think of a place he'd rather be than there, in that moment, with all the others crammed into Anna's cottage.

Anna called them inside for breakfast, and they gathered around the table in the tiny kitchen. For a second, everything felt as if it was back to normal as the sun rose over the town of Christchurch, and all seemed well with the sleepy little town.

ONE EVENING, Ruby brought a copy of the Amberley paper to Anna's. They laughed as she read aloud the story of a mysterious cult hidden behind the borders of a little town down the road from Amberley. As the police scoured the woods, they discovered several dozen bodies scattered through a town hidden in the center and a group locked away in a large meeting hall. Those who had survived were carted away to be interviewed. The story wove an intricate tapestry of murder, Satan worship, and mass suicide—most of it complete nonsense.

Obvious questions had arisen about how such a big town could have gone unnoticed, and several theories emerged, speculating that those in Christchurch had been involved somehow. The townsfolk had been brought in for questioning one by one, but all told the same consistent story, for the people of Christchurch knew the truth behind the secret town beyond the edge of the woods. They told the police of the existence of something—not magic, but not mundane either. But their stories didn't make it into the papers, and as with most extraordinary events that challenge the human understanding of the world, conspiracy theories and whispered rumors obscured the truth.

Oliver heard nothing more of the burned-out warehouse on the train tracks although he assumed the police had investigated it too.

The question remained of what to do since the Collector had burned Izzy's house to the ground. Anna's tiny cottage being packed with four humans and two animals was an unsustainable solution for the long term.

A few days later, Oliver crossed the square past the market and headed down the dirt road to where Izzy's house had been. He found her in the spot where the Briarwood Witch had flipped the police cruiser more than a year before, staring at the pile of charred wood.

Oliver approached and sat next to her on the grass. She didn't acknowledge him, so he sat with her for a moment in contemplative silence.

"We're getting ready to make dinner," he said. "Want to come back to the cottage with me?"

Her eyes snapped to him as she came back from her daydream. "Yeah, just sit here with me for another minute."

Oliver nodded. "Are you doing okay?"

She looked at him. "Okay? Not quite, but I'll get there. I'm just trying to figure out how I'll say goodbye."

"Goodbye?"

"I talked to the insurance people today. They're sending the check in the mail. Told me how much it would be for, and I practically lost it right there on the phone with... Larry was his name, I think."

"Is it enough to rebuild the place?" Oliver asked.

Izzy hesitated. "It's enough," she said. "But I had other ideas in mind."

"Really?"

"The house had gotten too big for me, anyway. I can barely climb up the stairs, and it's so much to clean, even with your help."

"You really are a glass-half-full kind of person, aren't you?" he asked. "Your house burns down, and you're listing off all the reasons you're happy about it." He grinned.

"I can't help it. I've been thinking about it for a while, though. And now that I have the money, we could have the rest of this plowed over, pay off the bakery, then I..."

"You what?" he asked.

"Could find a smaller place in the city. Maybe an apartment with an elevator. We could even open up another shop there. Anna's been working so hard at the bakery, and I've thought about making her co-owner. I've always dreamt of living in Amberley, and with this kind of money—"

"What about the bees?"

"If we clean up the house, we can use all this extra space for more hives. You've been getting better at taking care of the little buggers. There are plenty of wildflowers down in the field for them. We'd be swimming in honey and beeswax!"

Oliver shook his head to clear his mind of the mental image.

"I'm serious. Maybe you could run the hives or help me set up a new bakery in Amberley."

Oliver sat back and looked at the rubble in front of them. When he laid his eyes on Izzy's house for the first time in a decade, the cheery yellow siding had lifted his spirits, and the place soon felt like home. But after a while, he realized home was more than a place—home was a feeling that came with family and friendships. Clearly, Izzy had realized this a long time before.

"I guess it was only a matter of time before I'd have to find a place of my own."

"You ought to give Amberley a shot. We can look together."

"What about Asher?"

"We'll figure something out," Izzy replied.

Although Oliver felt a knot in his stomach at the thought of finding his own apartment, he thought back to the ticking clock that had sent him to Christchurch. If he hadn't shattered that clock, he might not have even made it to Christchurch. When Izzy's place burned, another clock had overturned, and he would take advantage of all the opportunities for change and growth that would come along with the new challenge.

"Shall we get back, kiddo?" she asked.

Oliver nodded.

She looked at the crushed station wagon underneath the collapsed porte cochere. "I'm having a run of bad luck with station wagons," she said. "Maybe I should go with a more conventional car this time around. Perhaps a delivery van would be the best thing after all."

Oliver grimaced. "I can't let you do that. If we need a delivery van, too, that's fine, but a painted station wagon is a tradition now."

Izzy looked at him. "And you know how much I *value* tradition," she replied.

"Good point."

They took the road back toward the town square. As Izzy and Oliver walked past the buildings of Christchurch, Oliver thought back to his first day in town, stumbling through the square with Nekko in a duffel bag on his shoulder, wondering what life had in store for him. Little did he know then that the town held his future and the closest family he would ever know. Now, he would have to move on to the next adventure, but this time, he wouldn't have to do it alone.

ENJOY THE BOOK?

Please Consider Leaving a Review

Reviews help tremendously. Please consider leaving a
review on Amazon or Goodreads!

Check Out Chris Cooper's Standalone Novel

The Dreadful Objects

Want More Oliver Crum Books? Find an Error?

Let us know or join our mailing list at Dreadfulmedia.com.

ABOUT THE AUTHOR

Chris Cooper is a writer, college professor, novice coffee roaster, and recovering engineer. He lived and worked in Japan, where he developed an obscure obsession for fancy fountain pens and currently lives in Ohio with his partner and Australian Cattle Terrier. Both enjoy going for walks. Chris writes supernatural thrillers full of colorful three-dimensional characters, macabre adventures, and twisty turny plots.